Born and educa … has been writing
steadily for the … in
many translati… . He
has written wi… ht and
is often consul… .

An ex-editor, … e
Fiction Assoc… Trieste
Festival and was chosen to be guest of hono… rld
Science Fiction Convention at Heidelberg. His studies embrace astronomy, physics and extra-sensory perception while his hobbies include photography, ancient weapons and archaeology.

Also available in the *Space 1999* series

BREAKAWAY by E. C. Tubb
MOON ODYSSEY by John Rankine
THE SPACE GUARDIANS by Brian Ball
COLLISION COURSE by E. C. Tubb
LUNAR ATTACK by John Rankine
ASTRAL QUEST by John Rankine
ALIEN SEED by E. C. Tubb
ANDROID PLANET by John Rankine

E. C. Tubb

Space 1999: Rogue Planet

Futura Publications Limited
An Orbit Book

To: Rita Jane Lawrence

An Orbit Book
First published in Great Britain in 1976
by Futura Publications Limited

ISBN 0 8600 7926 0

Printed in Great Britain by
Hazell Watson & Viney Ltd
Aylesbury, Bucks

Futura Publications Limited
110 Warner Road
Camberwell, London SE5

CHAPTER ONE

There were times when John Koenig wished that more than Earth had been left behind when, on that black day in September 1999, the Moon had blasted free from its age-old orbit to begin its fantastic journey through the universe. There were irritations and annoyances he could have done without and, at the moment, Sarah Pulcher was the worst.

'Commander!' she gushed. 'I need you. We all need you. Please?'

'No.'

'But if you would only reconsider. You would be ideal for the part.'

'No,' snapped Koenig again, then softened the harshness of his tone a little. Sarah Pulcher wasn't really bad, she was just a dedicated idealist determined to get her own way; a trait he could appreciate. 'You don't need me, Sarah. From what I hear you've a superb company and I'm sure you'll put on a magnificent performance.'

If not it wouldn't be because of failure on her part but, looking at the dark intensity of Koenig's face; the sweep of black hair, the eyes, the sensitivity of the mouth, the firmness of the jaw, it was hard not to feel regret. He would have made a perfect Hamlet. Tall, a little too old for accurate representation, perhaps, but his added maturity would have given a greater depth to the role. And, too, the presence of the Commander would have guaranteed success.

Watching her, guessing her thoughts, Koenig inwardly smiled. Odd talents had appeared among the personnel of Moonbase Alpha once they had been irrevocably divorced from their home world. Artists had appeared among them, sculptors, musicians, actors, but who would have guessed that the short, dumpy woman now standing before him would have blossomed into a producer of Shakespearian plays? From the treasured books and folios in her room it was obvious that she was a dedicated follower of the Bard and was now, in a sense, achieving a life-long ambition.

'Commander?' She had been studying his face, catching the slight, almost imperceptible movement of muscle and tissue, reading the interplay of intent and emotion. 'You don't object?'

'To the play? Of course not.'

'I was thinking of my request, Commander. Have you decided?'

That was another matter. Sarah Pulcher was an organic chemist and as such of more value to the base than any producer of plays. Yet men could not live on bread alone. They had to be given periods of recreation and the opportunity to relax. The theatre was a new project and could provide the essential ingredient of actual participation which recordings, no matter how good, could not. Actors and audience, interchanging roles, maintaining a dialogue, building the family-like affinity the Alphans must have if they hoped to survive.

And, to be happy and content, it was essential to ensure job-satisfaction. The woman would do her job as before should he insist but, subconsciously, she would be resentful and prone to error.

Koenig said, 'You're important to us in more ways than one, Sarah. Alpha can't afford to lose your skills. If—'

'My assistant is perfectly capable of conducting the routine, Commander,' she said quickly. 'And I will always be available. I promise that you will have no reason to regret granting my request.' And then she added, with almost frightening intensity, 'Please, Commander. Please!'

A cruel man or a sadistic one would have kept her on a hook, but Koenig was neither. A stupid one would have rejected her application, blind to the long-term advantages, but no fool would ever have gained the command of Moonbase Alpha and no stupid man could ever have held that command once they had plunged deep into the unknown.

Sitting back in his chair Koenig smiled. 'It's yours, Sarah. As from this moment you are the official head of the theatre company. But I warn you, you'll have to be good or someone will be after your job.'

'If I'm not good they will have the right to take it.' She returned his smile; a woman glowing with happiness. 'Are you positive you won't take part, Commander?'

'No.'

'Not even a small one? I could arrange—'

'If you keep tormenting me, woman, I'll have you put in chains!' His scowl accentuated the mock anger of his voice, a display which confirmed her belief in his acting abilities. 'Now move!'

'Yes, my lord. At once, my lord.' She made a curtsey, as mocking as his feigned rage, a gesture which seemed to bring with it the rustle of billowing skirts, the dance of candlelight, the grace of a departed age. 'Until the first night then, my lord. I shall see that you get one of the best seats.'

He rose as she left, stretching, feeling pleasure at happiness given, warmed by the woman's radiated joy. Aiming his commlock he opened the wide doors and stepped into the ordered activity of Main Mission.

As always he looked at the screens.

They showed the space lying ahead, the area into which the Moon was relentlessly moving. A great emptiness dotted with the gleam of a multitude of stars, glowing points of distant brilliance, the sheets and curtains of hazy luminescence, the blurred fuzz of remote nebulae. An awe-inspiring spectacle which always gripped him and made him conscious of the relative insignificance of Mankind. Tiny creatures living on a mote of dust lost in the tremendous vastness of the universe. Even on their own planet they had been minute – now, adrift on what had been their satellite they were poised on the very edge of extinction.

But they had minds and intelligence and the will to survive.

They were human and they were of Earth.

'Nothing, Commander.' Sandra Benes reported from where she sat at her instruments, answering the question in his eyes as he looked at her. 'Space registers empty as far as we can scan.'

'Kano?'

'Computer verifies.' He touched the bulk of his charge. 'All extrapolations show an absence of any form of potential danger.'

'Good.' Koenig felt himself relax even more. It would be good simply to concentrate on the inner workings of Alpha, to plot new lines of activity, to forge ahead with expension and construction. And all without the need of strain or urgency. The play had come at a good time.

Paul Morrow mentioned it from where he sat at the main consol.

'Did you decide about Sarah Pulcher, Commander?'

'Yes.'

'And?'

'I've given her the go-ahead. There seemed no harm in it and she's earned the chance.'

'She's certainly worked on that play of hers,' said Paul. 'Every spare moment she's had she's been working on costumes and make-up and all the rest of it. Right, Sandra?'

'That is right, Paul.'

'I said she should try for a part. She would make a fine Desdemona, right, David?'

Kano smiled with a display of teeth startlingly white against the rich brownness of his skin. 'That's right,' he agreed. And I'd make a good Othello.'

'The best. And you, Commander? What part do you fancy?'

The part of Moses, of bringing his people home safe from the wilderness, but Koenig didn't say so.

From where he lay on the bed Sam Blake could see the edge of the desk, the rounded curve of a shoulder and the glint of a helmet of blonde hair. A careless nurse had left the door of the ward open and so provided him with a view, but intriguing as it was he would willingly have changed it for another, far more bleak, perhaps, but also far more familiar.

'Sam?' Tony Ellman occupying a bed opposite lifted his head from the pillow. 'Can you see if she's moving?'

'She isn't.'

'When she does, wave at her. Attract her attention in some way. I want to get out of here.'

'Who doesn't?' Sam moved, cursing his leg, the inattention which had sent him toppling into a shallow crevass to land awkwardly, to send him to Medical with a broken shin. 'They've fitted Stader's,' he said, bitterly. 'The bone's reinforced with metal plates and still they keep me cooped up in bed like a sick child. Doctor!'

At the desk the woman stirred.

'Doctor Russell!' yelled Sam again. 'Here, please!'

Helena lifted her head and sat for a moment deciding whether or not to answer the call. The patient was in no danger and she could guess what he wanted.

'Doctor!'

Sighing Helena Russell moved a heap of papers to one side and rose. A nurse could have answered the call and would have done so had she summoned one, but the girl on duty was probably engrossed and the others would be equally engaged. And, as she had cause to remember, Sam Blake had an overpowering manner. It took experience to be able to handle an aggressive male patient and the conflict would provide a welcome distraction from the statistics she had been studying.

'Doctor Russell!' Sam smiled at her as she entered the ward. Big, strong, muscles toughened by long and arduous labour, he bulked huge beneath the covers. The hood lifting the sheet off the injured leg gave him a lop-sided appearance. With an easy movement he lifted himself so as to sit upright in the bed. 'Doctor, when do I get out of here?'

'And me, Doctor.' Tony Ellman, smaller but just as pugnacious in his way, didn't intend to be ignored. 'I've work to do and it won't get done with me lying here. How about it?'

'I've one answer for the pair of you,' she said, flatly. 'No.'

'No?' Sam frowned. 'No, what?'

'No, you can't get up, you can't get out, you can't return to duty.' Helena lifted the board from the foot of the bed. 'Now listen to this, Sam Blake. You were brought in here from outside suffering from a broken shin, multiple contusions, slight narcosis and shock. In fact you are lucky to be alive. I intend to keep you that way given a little help.'

'I feel fine.'

'Of course. You've been drugged so as to eliminate pain. You've had a long rest under electro-sleep. Glucose and saline has been fed into your veins. The broken bone has been treated and, when the wound heals, you'll be as good as new. But not yet.'

'Why not, Doctor?' He scowled. 'Look, I feel just fine and I should know. I can get up this very moment. Damn it, Doctor, why the hell do I have to stay here in bed like some broken down cripple?'

Helena said, coldly, 'What is your job, Blake?'

'What?' Her sudden chill had startled him. 'I'm a technician. I work outside mostly, checking for fissures and maintaining the scanners. Why?'

'Do I try to teach you your job?'

'No, but—'

'Then don't try to teach me mine. If you want to get up then go ahead. Your leg might take what you intend to give it, but on the other hand it might not. The wound could become infected and that could lead to amputation.' Helena glanced at the board. 'I see you're fond of gymnastics – lose a leg and you'll have to find another hobby. But that's up to you. If you want to take the chance go ahead.' Her tone chilled even more. 'But remember this – discharge yourself and you're on your own. Don't come whining back to me for help if things go wrong. Well?'

She was bluffing; never would she permit any patient to leave unless he was a hundred per cent fit and certainly she would never withold medical aid to any who might need it, but Blake didn't know that and couldn't afford to take the chance. He lay silent for a moment, thinking, remembering how dependent he and every other Alphan was on the sole source of medical assistance, the skill and dedication of the woman and her staff. And she had been right, as a technician he could appreciate that. Each to their own speciality.

'Well?' Ellman watched from across the room. 'What's it to be, Sam?'

'You wanted out too.'

'I know,' admitted the other man. 'Now I'm not so certain. How much longer will it be, Doctor?'

'For you another three days. For you,' she looked at Blake, 'a day extra. I want to make sure those sutures have taken. If there is any infection I want to catch it at once and, to be frank, I can't trust you to take things easy.' Warmth edged into her voice, a calculated intimacy to remove the sting from the metaphorical slap she had given. 'You big men are always hard to handle. At times I think you've never really grown up.' Then, casually she added, 'How close are you to becoming gymnastics champion?'

The question pleased him, removing the last of any irritation he might have felt, soothing any bruise to his pride.

'Close,' he said with a touch of pride. 'Webb's in the lead but I can wipe out his advantage as soon as I master the treble turn and flip. You should come and see me at work, Doctor. As a student of anatomy you could be interested.'

'In what?' snapped Ellman. 'In you, you big ape? The lady has more to do than inflate your ego. Anyway, you're inefficient, right, Doctor? His muscles burn too much oxygen and his bulk takes too much energy to move around. Yes?'

'That's a matter of opinion.'

'No it isn't.' He was quick to the attack. 'I've read about it and Peggy Moore verified it. She works in the hydroponic farms and she's a dietician. She told me all about the relative efficiency of fuel-intake to energy output and big, bulky men have a less efficient metabolism than, well, someone like me, for example.'

'Rubbish!'

'It isn't!' Ellman appealed to Helena. 'Aren't I right, Doctor? Tell that big ape I'm right.'

'No,' she said. 'Fight it out between yourselves – but the first one who moves an inch from his bed gets immobilised for a week. I mean that!'

A threat which would prevent any actual physical violence and restrain them to verbal battle. At least, for them, it would pass the time and ease boredom.

Helena leaned her back against the closed door and closed

her eyes. Always she had the nagging fear of the unknown and Blake's leg was a problem. The wound hadn't acted as it should which was the real reason she had kept him in bed. Stader's, correctly applied, mended the bone and allowed immediate movement of the affected limb. But, while the surgery had been without fault, the healing process was unaccountably slow.

An unsuspected result of prolonged exposure to the wild radiations of space, perhaps? An effect of working in the harsh and unfamiliar environment outside? Even the low gravity coupled with alien physical demands could have been a contributary factor.

There was so much they still had to learn.

'Doctor?' Mathias was walking towards her. Smiling he nodded at the closed door of the ward. 'Trouble?'

'An argument, that's all.'

'Serious?'

'No.' She took a deep breath and returned his smile. 'Just boredom, Bob, but I've taken care of it. Was there something?'

'Yes,' he said. 'It's time you were getting ready to attend the play.'

Koenig called for her, waiting as she fastened the flower he had brought to the shoulder of her uniform, a plastic thing yet one of delicate colour and form, bright with golden flecks against a background of smouldering scarlet.

'An orchid,' he said. 'At least I think it is. There are so many kinds you can never be sure.'

'Thank you, John.' She rested her hand on his arm, aware of the fine lines of strain marking his face, the added tension creasing the flesh at the corners of his eyes. An older face than he had worn when first taking over the command of Moonbase, one which had seen more than its share of death and danger, of the pit which waited, ever-hungry, at the edge of the tiny world which they called their own.

'I should have brought chocolates,' he said. 'Sweets to the sweet, but they'd just sold the last box.'

'Just as well,' she said, entering into the spirit of the fantasy.

'They'd only put on extra inches. Well, Commander, are we ready?'

With a flourish he extended his arm. 'Yes, my lady, let us now go to witness the trials and tribulations of a most unhappy prince of Denmark.'

And to witness just what Sarah Pulcher had managed to accomplish.

As far as Koenig could see the woman couldn't be faulted. As he guided Helena to her seat in the auditorium he studied the ceiling and walls. The place had been gouged from the Lunar rock, the stone smoothed and polished, panels set up together with lights and decorations so that the area was reminiscent of the great theatres of Europe. Naturally there were differences, no Royal Box for one and no serried tiers, no orchestra pit either and no heavy proscenium, but the general atmosphere had been captured and held. Here was a place in which make-believe would find a home. A shrine dedicated to the art of mime and gesture, of words and song, of graceful shapes and monsters moving through the intricacies of an artificial world.

Habit made Koenig reach for his commlock.

'Paul?'

Morrow's face looked from the tiny screen. He, along with others, remained on duty; a skeleton staff which maintained observation. 'Commander?'

'All well?'

'Everything is under control,' Morrow assured. 'Space is as empty as far as we can scan. All systems functioning on optimum level. Don't worry, Commander. Relax and enjoy yourself.'

And don't keep bothering me, thought Koenig, adding the unspoken comment. Unfairly, perhaps, but he could guess how the other felt and knew that he had made a mistake in making the check. Unless subordinates were shown they were trusted they would become unfitted for trust.

'John?' Helena smiled at him as he took his place at her side. 'Trouble?'

'No, just making a routine check. How is your section?'

'Bob can handle it,' she said, firmly. 'This is the first play I've had the chance to see since we left Earth and I'm not going to spoil it. Now relax, John, and forget duty for a while.'

Something he could never do but for a few hours at least he could push it deep into the back of his mind. And the atmosphere of the theatre helped. At the chime of a bell the lights began to lower and a blur of light and shadow drifted across the curtain. Music filled the air, soft, the throb and pulse of tambours and sackbuts, of flutes and horns. Music which augmented the illusion of being carried back in time to another world, another place.

The curtains opened and they looked at Elsinore.

It was magic, thought Koenig. The art of the illusionist, scenes created from light and shadow, props, plaster, paint and suggestion. Bergman had helped and would even now be behind the scenes busy with his electronic wizardry, but the setting, the atmosphere, the choice of the men who now appeared in costume, all were a tribute to the skill and dedication of Sarah Pulcher who had taken words and directions and had made them come alive and real.

The genius of William Shakespeare presented by the most unusual travelling company of players ever to have trod a board.

With a contented sigh Koenig relaxed and sank into the illusive and famous world of the Baird.

There had, he knew, been better productions of the play but he doubted if any had been more eagerly received by an audience which surely was the most receptive there could be. The actors too, a little rough, perhaps, but gaining confidence as the minutes passed, their roughness adding to rather than detracting from their roles. Francisco, Bernardo, Horatio and Marcellus. The King was a giant, his Queen a mature accompaniment, Hamlet himself a tall figure of incipient madness, flashes of paranoia merged with the bitter necessity of acceptance, the frustration of thwarted desire.

'Clever, whispered Helena at his side. 'Sarah was shrewd to illuminate the incestuous desire of the son for the mother and to be able to bring it across so soon.'

'Hamlet for Gertrude? The Oedipus Complex?'

'Yes – it's obvious when you have the clue and Sarah's managed to leave it in no doubt. Remember Hamlet hates his uncle but as yet has no knowledge of his guilt as a murderer. The hate, as such, is illogical unless we accept the strong sexual motivation which drives it. Once that is accepted all the rest falls into place. The revelations of the ghost simply provide an excuse and justification for revenge.' Her hand closed tightly on his arm. 'Hush, now. Here it comes.'

The curtains parted for Scene V and the prince's communication with the ghost of his murdered father. Mist trailed across the platform, dimming the appearance of detail, the distant figures, barely observed of waiting attendants. Hamlet was in the foreground, a cunningly aimed spotlight illuminating his features with a pale, nacreous glow, not too dim to take the attention from the disturbingly frightening appearance of the apparition he faced.

Somewhere in Koenig's brain a connection was made and, suddenly, he was a boy again, sitting in a classroom, mouthing words by rote; taking the part of the ghost.

> 'I am thy father's spirit;
> Doomed for a certain term to walk the night,
> And for the day confin'd to fast in fires,
> Till the foul crimes done in my days of nature
> Are burnt and purged away. But that I am forbid
> To tell the secrets of my prison-house,
> I could a tale unfold....'

A spirit condemned to eternal suffering for the sake of sins unshriven, a relic of a time when men believed in the punishment which waited after death to sear and corrode all who had not kept the Faith.

Koenig blinked, narrowing his eyes as he watched the ghost. Bergman's magic was superb. The thing seemed almost transparent, the gleam of a subdued torch showing through the rotting shroud. The voice itself, booming, sepulchral, grated on ears and nerves and sent little chills running up his spine. A voice augmented by the use of sub-sonics, he guessed, bolstered by a selection of vibratory frequencies designed to activate the fear-centres of the brain.

Turning he whispered, 'Helena—'

'Hush!' Her tone was savage. 'Listen, John. Listen!'

The ghost again.

> 'O Hamlet! what a falling-off was there;
> From me, whose love was of that dignity
> That it went hand in hand even with the vow
> I made to her in marriage; and to decline
> Upon a wretch whose natural gifts were poor
> To those of mine!'

Helena was entranced as were all in the auditorium. Glancing around Koenig could see the rapt faces and unwinking eyes, feeling the strained tension as if it were a tangible thing, almost tasting the sheer concentration directed at the stage. They were enamoured, entrapped, caught in the illusion of the play.

Sarah Pulcher could have received no better accolade.

From the stage the eerie voice continued, lifting, throbbing, demanding full attention. A grim voice, chill in its condemnation, ruthlessly twisting a nature already warped. The hand of the dead reaching out to ruin the lives of those left behind.

> 'Thus was I, sleeping, by a brother's hand,
> Of life, or crown, of queen, at once dispatched,
> Cut off even in the blossoms of my sin,
> Unhousel'd, disappointed, unanel'd,
> No reckoning made, but sent to my account
> With all my imperfections on my head;
> O, horrible! O, horrible!
> Move not ahead on this thy present path to ruin,
> But retreat! Withdraw! Return!
> Yield unto the necessity of the time,
> Go! Leave! Move not into peril!
> Turn back! Back! Back!'

Words never written by the Bard and which never should have been uttered in such a context. Koenig felt Helena stiffen at his side, heard the sudden hum from the audience. Some, a very few, unfamiliar with the play had spotted nothing amiss. Others had.

'Those words!' Helena looked at Koenig. 'They don't belong. John, what is Victor playing at?'

'Maybe the ghost got out of hand?' Koenig glanced at the stage. 'Look! It's changing!'

The scabrous image of rotting shroud and leprous flesh dissolved into something tall and regal. One arm lifted and the face, wreathed by a full, white beard, tilted, illuminated by an inward light.

'Halt! Take warning! You are about to enter a region of space containing extreme danger. Retreat while you are able. Nothing but fear and destruction lies ahead. You will know only devastation and death. Retreat! Return! Withdraw! You have been warned!'

The figure swelled, dissolving, emitting a wave of almost tangible dread, an emotion which caused men to cry out and women to scream as they cowered in their seats hiding their eyes, their ears.

Victims of the panic which ruled the entire base.

CHAPTER TWO

Professor Victor Bergman was an old man with a high forehead and a mechanical heart which had given him life and, so some hinted, had robbed him of all human emotion. A lie as Koenig well knew, the device had extended a valuable life and had given an already clear brain an even greater clarity, but intelligent as that brain was it found itself baffled.

'I don't understand it, John. All the scanners report only negative results. There was certainly no massive electromagnetic energy field which affected our life-support systems. If the evidence wasn't against it I'd say that it was the result of a simple mass-hysteria caused by a careless use of sonic stimulators.'

'And it isn't?'

'No, John.' Bergman shook his head to emphasise the point. 'Their range was strictly limited. In any case the projection would never have been able to penetrate the rock surrounding the auditorium and, as we know, the panic was one which encompassed the base.'

'Helena?'

'It was a feeling, John,' she reported. 'A wave of sudden, inexplicable terror which momentarily disorganised the entire personnel of Alpha. All agree on certain points; the desire to run, to hide, to withdraw. Fortunately it didn't last long enough to endanger anyone.'

'No visual stimuli?'

For a moment she hesitated then said, 'Not that anyone will admit to. As far as it goes those in the auditorium are the only ones who actually saw anything unusual. And not everyone will admit to that now.'

A self-protective refusal to accept the evidence of their own senses and a natural one. Hallucinations were always worrisome and no one would be willing to admit they suffered from them. And yet Koenig had no doubt as to what he had seen and heard.

Neither had Helena but Bergman, oddly, had less certainty.

'I was in the projection booth,' he explained. 'As you know the ghost was a hologram projected on a cloud of controlled vapour – we used a gas with a high metallic content and managed to shape and move it by the use of powerful magnetic fields. Rather effective, do you agree?'

'Wonderful,' said Koenig dryly. 'But the voice?'

'Projected through electronic filters. The sonic emitters were set facing the auditorium, of course. The strength of projection was two degrees above the lower level of conscious awareness. An application of sub-liminal influence, you understand.' He broke off, coughing, suddenly aware that he had been rambling. 'I'm sorry to be a poor witness, John, but if we caused what happened then I am totally unaware of how it was done. The energies involved simply don't lend themselves to such a conclusion.'

'What you are saying is that what happened could not have been caused by any actions of our own. Is that it?'

Bergman drew in his breath. 'Yes, John. That is what I'm saying.'

'Helena?'

'I've checked Victor's figures as far as I'm able and I must agree with him,' she said. 'Certainly the sonic projectors could never have affected the entire base and we do know that all personnel experienced the sudden emotional panic though in a greater or lesser degree. The node seems to have been the auditorium. It was also the point of greatest visual derrangement – at least more people were willing to admit they saw something there than anywhere else.'

'And the words?' Koenig stared from one to the other as neither made comment. 'I take it that we did hear the words?'

'We did, John, yes,' admitted Helena.

'We? You mean you and I? How about the others? Victor?'

Koenig frowned as Bergman shook his head. They had met in his office, the wide doors leading to Main Mission now closed. Rising from behind his desk he crossed the floor with short, impatient strides. The lines of his face were deep, the contours set in rigid planes.

He said, curtly, 'There's a mystery here and I want to solve it. A fictional ghost turns into a bearded prophet and—'

'Bearded?' Helena looked startled. 'John, that figure didn't have a beard. It was clean-shaven and wore a dress suit with a decoration of some kind.'

'It was bearded,' said Koenig. 'At least the thing I saw had a beard and a robe of some kind. You say it wasn't – which means?'

'If the both of you looked at the same thing and each saw a different image then there is only one thing it can mean.' Bergman was positive. 'What you saw was subjective, not objective. In other words it wasn't really there, you only imagined it was.'

'Helena?'

'I agree with Victor. It is the only way to explain the differing reports I've received. Even accounting for hysteria and natural diversity in recounting a traumatic experience there is too much divergence. Some are too vague to be even logical, others mention octapoid and polypoidal creatures as if they were recounting the stuff of nightmare. Nonsense, of course, but illuminating.'

'Nightmare,' said Koenig. He looked at his left hand, the fingers were clenched and, deliberately, he forced himself to spread them, flexing them, easing the tension, masking the fear they had betrayed. 'We each saw something, a creature of authority or nightmare which could, psychologically, mean the same thing. Most of us, in our time, have been scared by authority so it is merely a transference of symbols. Never mind that for the moment. Let's take a look at what we have. Something, some external force, caused a form of mass hallucination. Right?'

'Until we have a better explanation, John, that will serve as a working hypothesis,' said Bergman. 'Helena?'

'I agree.'

'The next question,' said Koenig, grimly, 'Is just what the hell caused it. And how?'

'What I don't know,' said Helena. 'But I can take a guess as to how. I think it was done, or caused, by direct stimulation of the brain. Normally we see something and the image is carried via the optic nerve to the brain where it is resolved into a recognisable shape and subject. Now, if we stimulate the correct centres of the brain the reverse can happen. A subject can be made to see something which isn't actually there. The same applies to hearing, of course. In fact I can produce exactly those results in my laboratory.'

'By hypnotism?' Bergman was interested.

'That is one method, but I was thinking of electrical cortical stimulation with the use of probes.'

'Hypnotism,' said Koenig. Returning to the desk he leaned on it, resting the flats of both hands on the surface. 'We were entranced, enamoured, concentrating on the play. Everyone was. The ghost was a shifting, flickering image, exactly what would lead to a hypnotic trance-condition. Am I making sense?'

'Yes and no,' said Helena. 'Our concentration would have made us vulnerable to group suggestion and equally so to response to cortical stimulation, but we can rule out simple hypnotism. There would have had to be a director or directive of some kind. A prompter to tell us what to see. And you are forgetting the words.'

The warning. Koenig straightened and glanced towards the closed doors. Beyond them, he knew, sensitive instruments were sending their findings to digital readouts, to dials, to shifting graphs all to be studied and correlated by skilled personnel and the mammoth abilities of the computer. Yet despite all their skill and technology, they had found nothing.

'Halt,' he said, thickly. 'Retreat. Withdraw. Return. Death and devastation lie ahead. Did you all get it?'

'In one form or another, yes.' Helena touched the fullness of her lower lip with the tip of her tongue as if even thinking of the episode had dried the natural saliva. 'It could be a natural accompaniment to the hallucination. We are afraid of what could lie ahead and we would all like to return, to go back, to be safe.'

An answer, but not a good one; the mystery remained and with it the fear and anxiety. Koenig didn't believe in natural happenings, for each event there had to be a reason and to find explanations in the realm of philosophical abstractions was to dodge the issue. At times such dodging was of no importance – on Earth, for example, odd accounts of strange sightings and inexplicable events had been dismissed or ignored without apparent detriment. But they were not on Earth. They had little or no reserves. A mistake, any mistake, could be the last they would make.

On the Moon there was simply no room for the unknown.

'Victor, run that projection again and repeat the sequence up and down forward and back with varying strengths of sonic projection. Ask for volunteers. I want to check there was no possibility that the occurrence wasn't of our own doing.'

'I've already checked, John.'

'Then do it again!' Koenig made no attempt to soften his tone. 'Helena, you do the same. Tests on all together with cross-questioning. Hypnotic recall if you think it necessary. With enough information we might come up with the true answer.'

'We may already have it,' she said, bleakly. 'We received a warning, remember?'

'Yes,' he said, harshly. 'To halt. To return. To withdraw. To go back. Now tell me how the hell we can possibly obey it!'

The bottle was half-empty and Sam Blake scowled at it remembering a joke he had once been told, a philosophical concept which hadn't amused him then and didn't now. A bottle half-empty was just that and calling it one half-full didn't alter the amount of the contents. Well, to hell with it, when it was all gone maybe he could get more or, at least, would be out of the ward, the bed, the whole damned prison the Medical Section had become.

Lifting the bottle he drank, swallowing the neat alcohol it contained; surgical spirit intended to ease the pain of bedsores, to clean surface areas of skin. A product of the yeast vats which helped to provide their food and which he had stolen to use as an anodyne for boredom.

He glowered at the lowered level and gently moved his injured leg. Days now and still the damned thing hadn't healed. Tony Ellman had gone, smiling, eager to get back to work, making a joke as he left to see about getting a crutch. A joke in bad taste – surely it couldn't come to that, a broken leg, a gash which was slow in healing.

Quickly he took another drink.

The nurse, damn her, had closed the door so that he couldn't see out of the ward and so was left in a form of solitary confinement foreign to his nature. He had always liked company, the boisterous comradeship of his fellow workers, the challenge of gymnastic activity. A big man, proud of his body, enjoying the euphoria of fitness, of using the fine engine of flesh and blood which was his own.

Again he moved his leg, wincing at the stab of pain. Throwing back the cover he examined it, frowning at the ugly red streaks running from the wound, the skin distended and tender. The doctors had seen it, had muttered over it, had filled him with antibiotics and other assorted junk all with no apparent success. Tomorrow, so he had heard, he was to be given a complete blood-change and after that, if necessary, immersion in an amniotic tank where new tissue would be grown to replace that they would have to cut away.

He wouldn't die and he wouldn't lose his leg but he would lose time and the championship would have been decided and he would still be in this or another ward fitted up with life-support mechanisms of one kind or another. Time which dragged past on leaden feet. Feet – the plural.

He took another drink.

And, remembering Ellman's parting joke, yet another and then, because it wasn't worth saving the little which remained, he emptied the bottle and sank back with his head on the pillow staring at the central light the ward contained.

A bright light which seemed to flicker and swell and pulse as if with a life of its own. To change even as he watched. To alter.

Mathias heard him scream.

He had been studying a tissue sample from the man's injured leg, frowning at the distortion of the cellular structure, testing a variety of agents and collating the results. The scream caught him as he was fitting a new slide and he swore as the glass shattered, a sliver cutting a finger so that blood dripped to stain the sterile instrument.

It came again as he straightened, a shriek which sounded less than human, a thing compounded of naked terror and heart-stopping fear.

'Doctor!' A nurse came running towards him, her eyes enormous in the pallor of her face. 'It's Sam Blake. I—'

'Get help!' Mathias thrust past her, leaving a smear of blood from his cut hand on her uniform, the scarlet bright against the white sleeve. 'Bring sedatives. Hurry!'

He heard the scream again as he reached the ward and flinging open the door he ran inside.

To see the figure crawling on the floor, face and one hand uplifted, jagged shards of broken glass held like a dagger towards the throat. A dagger which plunged even as he watched to release a fountain of ruby, a stream of blood from severed arteries which splashed on the wall and dappled the floor with a crimson rain.

'Seven injured,' reported Helena. 'Five in shock; two catatonic. And one dead.'

Koenig frowned, 'Dead?'

'Sam Blake. He killed himself with a broken bottle. Bob saw him do it. Of the injured two are hospitalised; one caught his hand in a drill press, the other was burned. The other injuries are superficial and caused by collisions.' She added, unnecessarily, 'Their panic caused them to run.'

And one to run further than most – right into the security of the grave. Koenig remembered the man, a fine worker who would be missed. Not the type he would have taken for wanting nerve, but when true panic struck who could guarantee their reactions?

Remembering he said, 'How is Bob now?'

'He is a doctor and a good one.'

'So?'

'A doctor gets used to the sight of blood, John. He has to.'

And Mathias was a good doctor – which said nothing about his potential human weakness and, doctor or not, he could have succumbed to the general panic as had the rest. Koenig drew in his breath, remembering a time of nightmare when fear had clogged his veins and he had cringed with the desire to run, to escape, to hide.

If he had been weak and worried and afraid of personal hurt would he have yielded as Blake had done?

Or was it that the man had owned a far more intense imagination?

Questions, always questions, and still there were no answers. Bleakly he looked at the screens in Main Mission again seeing nothing but the cold burn of distant stars.

'Sandra?'

'Nothing, Commander.' She knew the implication of his call. 'Space, as far as all instrumentation is concerned, is totally empty ahead of us.'

'Kano, as far as computer is concerned, what are the extrapolations?'

'None, Commander. There is insufficient data on which computer can work.'

Koenig felt the fingers of his left hand beginning to close. It was useless to blame a machine for not having the intuitive faculty of a man – but how much data did the damn thing need?

'Try again,' he ordered. 'Feed it all the information we have and, if nothing else, obtain an intelligent guess.' An inconsistency, no machine could be intelligent despite the claims of those who served them, but Kano might find some factor he had previously overlooked. With relief he saw Bergman enter Main Mission. 'Victor! Anything?'

'Yes, but all negative.' Bergman cleared his throat. 'At least we can eliminate all thought of internal causes for the recent wave of panic. All equipment in the theatre was out of operation. I've checked all sources of electronic usage and none show any surge or loss which means we can eliminate all packets of energy-source such as spacial vortexes which could have created a high-order energy flow.'

'Which could mean that nothing happened and we have one dead man and several others injured for no reason at all.'

Koenig was being sarcastic and Bergman knew it. Quietly he said, 'There has to be a reason, John. All we've done so far is to eliminate sources of familiar energy, but there are others and they may be the cause.'

'Such as?'

'Victor is thinking of the paraphysical, John,' said Helena. 'We know that some people possess the talent to move objects without physical contact but as yet we have no means of discovering what type of energy they use. Telepathy, also, requires a form of energy and that is equally unexplained even though we know that telepathy exists. The warning—'

'Warning?'

'It has to be that,' she insisted. 'Twice now we have known panic and the desire to run. The first time we heard, or thought we heard, an actual voice giving us instructions. Perhaps that was because of the unusual conditions in which we received the message.'

And a man lay dead to show it should not be ignored.

Koenig took a step forward and halted just behind where Morrow sat at the main consol. Before him lamps flashed in endless signalling, one of the circuits which continually monitored the base and surround.

'The big screen, Paul. Full magnification.'

Koenig watched as the distant stars seemed to move aside, an optical illusion which gave the impression of hurtling at a fantastic velocity towards them in space. And still he saw nothing.

'Try filters.'

The stars flickered and changed colour as Morrow obeyed, feeding selective filters over the scanners, blocking out various bands of the electro-magnetic spectrum while bolstering others.

The results were the same.

Nothing.

Space remained as empty as before.

Empty, but holding something which had warned them twice now to stay away. Something which could emit psychic energy to directly influence the brain. A power which warned of devastation and death unless they obeyed.

But they could not obey.

The Moon was on a set course. The Alphans had no means of manoeuvring. No way they could dodge or slow, retreat or withdraw.

They could do nothing but hurtle on to whatever waited ahead.

'Commander?'

'That's enough, Paul. Order an Eagle and crew to make ready for an investigation-flight. Carter will want to take command – let him pick his own co-pilot.'

'And?'

'Put the base on yellow alert – and keep it on until further orders!'

CHAPTER THREE

Leaning back in the co-pilot's seat Ivor Khokol indulged in a dream. He was a chief of the Bandhaisai riding with Attila, the Kagan of the Hiung. Beneath the hooves of his horse the Steppes rolled back to the East while ahead, misted in rumour, lay the wealth of a decadent civilisation. Soon now they would reach the gates of Rome and the world would be theirs to loot, to burn, to take and use as they wished.

Even the thought of it sent the blood pounding in his veins to throb in his ears, sending adrenalin to stimulate nerve and muscle, sharpening his awareness, his aggression. The physical prelude to combat as it was a symptom of fear.

'Ivor!' From the pilot's chair Alan Carter glanced at his companion. 'Keep alert there!'

'I'm alert, Skipper.'

'Then report on instrumentation during the past five minutes.'

'All systems operating at optimum,' said Ivor immedately. 'Temperature of rear left lifting jet a little high but within tolerance. All clear on scanners. Radio contact at constant level. Humidity—'

'That's enough.' Automatically Carter scanned his own instrument panel, a shift of the eyes which had become second nature to the Head of Reconnaissance. Ahead space, as far as he could determine, was clear. As clear as it had been when they left Alpha an hour ago.

Settling back he thought about his co-pilot.

Ivor Khokol was a dreamer and a romantic of the old tradition, living in imagination the glories of the past, fighting ancient battles and adopting the mantle of the great. In that there was no harm, only when it threatened his efficiency would there be cause to worry. His immediate report had meant little; any serious fluctuation in the operation of the Eagle would have triggered an alarm and in such a case Carter would have acted.

Yet he hadn't actually lied, he had the facility of split-mind operation; turning a part of himself into a watchful automaton while allowing the rest of his mind to indulge in fantasies.

A trait which could be an asset in certain conditions but dangerous in others. No pilot, Carter knew, could be expected to maintain total concentration for long periods at a time. It was mentally and physically impossible to do that; insidious fatigue would ruin finely balanced judgements and, unless recognised, would lead to fatal error. A man who could watch for hours at a stretch, who would spring into full and complete awareness at any moment when triggered by something wrong, was a man ideal for routine patrols.

But for an investigation flight?

Carter had made his decision and had chosen Khokol to accompany him. How he acted now would determine his future with Reconnaissance.

He said, 'Skipper, have you ever studied history? I mean really studied it?'

'Why?'

'I was thinking of Attila. Of how he managed to unite the tribes and sweep across plains to reach Eastern Europe. You know that he actually managed to reach Rome and would have taken it if they hadn't bought him off.'

'So?'

'Think of it! A man, a barbarian in a sense, who managed to do the near-impossible. He could have made himself Emperor, become a Caesar, ruled the entire known world!'

'Instead of which,' said Carter, dryly, 'he died in pain to be burned by his followers. And after?'

'Nothing,' admitted Ivor. 'He was a strong man and there was no one to follow him. All he had built vanished almost at once. The affiliated tribes, the vassal Germanic peoples, all those who had become one force beneath his horsetail standard, all dissolved as snow in the sun. But if he had lived another ten years, or if he had managed to leave a strong heir, or if the tribes had managed to work together instead of letting petty feuds destroy their unity – who knows?'

'If pigs had wings they would fly.' Carter scanned the instrument and threw a switch. 'Eagle One to Main Mission. Paul?'

'Receiving.' Morrow's face appeared on the screen. 'Anything as yet, Alan?'

'No. We could be flying into a vacuum.'

'You are.'

'I was talking metaphorically. There's nothing out here but nothing.'

'Which is the way we want it to be.' Morrow smiled. 'Maintain alignment, Alan. It's important.'

'Will do.'

The screen went blank as Carter broke the connection and again he checked his instruments. The target-star was a fraction out and he returned it to the centre of the crosshairs with a deft touch on the controls. It was a big, blue-white sun and it could have planets and if so maybe they would pass close enough to investigate and, if any of those worlds could support life, they might find a new home.

If – always if.

Carter glanced around the command module of the Eagle, wondering if and when they finally found somewhere to stay and Operation Exodus was completed, what he would do. Fly, naturally, he could think of nothing else, but planetary flight would be odd after traversing the vast immensity of space, setting his course by the stars, lancing out from the Moon to check and probe and discover what there was to be discovered.

And every journey was a circle – each time he returned to Alpha.

There was no other place to go.

'Skipper!'

'What?'

'I – nothing.' Ivor frowned at the instruments. 'I thought I saw a flicker just then. One of the receptors registered. At least I thought it did.'

Dreaming or not he would have caught it and it was proof of his efficiency that Carter had not. For a moment he hesitated, studying the instruments, then again made contact with Alpha.

'Paul?'

'Here.' Morrow looked from the screen. 'Trouble?'

'Could be. Did you spot anything?'

'Such as?'

'An energy emission of some kind. One of the receptors kicked just now. No repetition as yet which could mean an internal malfunction or a local nexus of limited extent.'

'Nothing registered here, Alan.'

'Then it could be local, but you'd better maintain constant observation and monitoring. We could be heading into what we're looking for.'

Carter glared at what lay ahead. To the naked eye there was nothing, to the instruments the same, yet something was waiting there, he sensed it, felt it with every fibre of his being.

Grimly he resisted the urge to run. To turn the Eagle and head back to the Moon as fast as the ship would travel.

Ivor Khokol felt the same.

He shifted in his chair, easing his body against the restraints, his hands reaching for the controls only to fall back as he realised that to touch them would be useless. Carter had the control and would retain it unless there was a good reason why he should not. And a feeling, no matter how strong, was not reason enough for the Skipper to abandon his authority.

But, if he were dead?

An odd thought and Ivor did his best to banish it. He liked Carter and admired him and envied the man his skill and position. One day, with luck, he too would be a master-pilot with an Eagle of his own. One day, again with luck, he might reach up to become Head of a Section. One day.

He shivered, conscious of a sudden chill, then was suddenly gasping for breath. Blinking he stared ahead, concentrating on the stars, seeing them appear to shift and form new patterns. A house, a ship, a horse, the lineaments of a woman's face.

A smooth, firmly contoured visage with enigmatic eyes and a mouth which betrayed sensuality. Hollow cheeks and strong jaw. The hint of Slavic ancestry. The ears and blonde helmet of the hair.

Doctor Helena Russell!

Smiling at him from the empty depths of space.

Beckoning.

'No!' Alan Carter reared in his chair, snarling at the jerk of forgotten restraints, freeing them with a blow as he lunged towards his co-pilot. 'Don't, you fool! Don't!'

Ivor Khokol was already on his feet and reaching for the door of the module. His helmet was open and his eyes were glazed. One hand was resting on the control which would open the port – and beyond lay nothing but the airless void.

'Ivor!' Carter grabbed at his shoulder, turned the man, threw him back towards his chair. 'Seal up and strap down. That's an order!'

'I – no! I must go! I must!'

Madness. It showed in his face, his eyes, the tormented knotting of skin and muscles and, with the mania came a maniacal strength.

Carter was thrown back to crash against the hull head ringing from the impact, details blurring as he sank to his knees. Dazed, almost unconscious, he saw the other man tear at the portal, the sudden flood of ruby from the alarms, a red flush which accompanied the strident clangour of the warnings.

'Ivor! The controls!

'Too late!' The man turned, foam at his lips, blood running from bitten flesh. 'Wait for me! Please wait for me!'

Then there was nothing but a roar of confusion and an overwhelming darkness.

'Eighty-nine hours, seventeen minutes and thirty seconds as from – now!' Bergman threw the time-control on the chronometer then looked up from where he sat at his desk. 'That's how long it will take us to reach the same point as Alan did when he ran into trouble assuming, of course, that the area remains stationary relative to this region of space.'

'The Forbidden Area,' murmured Koenig. 'What caused the trouble, Victor? A barrier of some kind?'

'It could be that,' agreed the professor. 'And, coupled with the warnings, I think that it is. A final deterrent, the last warning before whatever lies behind the barrier is reached.'

And what that could be was anyone's guess. Restlessly

Koenig paced the room. Normally he liked to spend time in Bergman's laboratory, enjoying the touch of familiar things, seeing the rows of old books, the scrolls of proven accomplishment, the models and small items which Bergman had brought with him to the Moon back in the days when he had been a welcome visitor, an honoured guest granted the facilities of Moonbase Alpha to pursue his investigations.

Now there was no time to pause and linger, to step metaphorically back in time to when life was a matter of following routine instead of the continual challenge it had now become.

Pausing he stood before a chart hanging on the wall. It bore a mass of curves, symbols representing stars, a yellow swathe their progress. His finger rested on the point where the Moon was at the moment, moved on to halt at a red smear. Knowing their velocity any schoolboy could have computed the time remaining before they reached it, but no child born of woman could know what lay beyond.

'Did you manage to plot the extent of the area?'

'No.' Bergman shook his head as he came to stand beside Koenig. 'The only way would be to send out a series of Eagles and wait for something to happen. It would have taken too long.'

And have been too expensive on men. Koenig glared at the chart, feeling the anger of frustration. A known enemy he could have faced – but how to fight emptiness?

'Alan reported nothing visible as he approached the area,' he said. 'The monitoring verified his observations yet, as we know, something must lie in that region. What, Victor? A field of energy of some kind? A destructive vortex? A transdimensional warp?' His left hand made a fist. 'What the hell are we up against?'

Bergman said, thoughtfully, 'I'm not sure, John, but perhaps it is invisibility.'

'What?' Koenig shook his head. 'Invisible or not substance still has mass. It has temperature. It radiates energy. It can be spotted on instruments.'

'Not if it rested in a spherical field,' Bergman insisted. 'A bubble of force which rotates all received energy through a half-circle of 180 degrees. It is a mathematical concept, John, which we used to play with at university. How to become invisible. You can't do it by becoming transparent because any touch of dust or dirt will reveal you as it would a building made of glass. But if light could be rotated so that you saw not the object before you but the light it received from behind—'

'Then you wouldn't see it at all!' Koenig punched his right fist into his left hand. 'Of course. All light and so all visibility would be curved in a half-circle so that you would look around the object and not at it. The same would apply to all bands of the electro-magnetic spectrum. Our instruments are registering the energies received from beyond the area, the stars we see are really occluded but we can't tell that and so, for us, space ahead is empty. But how, Victor? Magnetic fields?'

'If so they must be of incredible density.' Bergman was dubious. 'It's possible, but I'm inclined to think a spacial warp of some kind could be responsible.'

Lifting the commlock from his belt Koenig snapped, 'Main Mission. Kano? Have the computer check on all stellar observations. I want special reference paid to any variation in apparent brightness or shift of position no matter how minute. Full scan in direction ahead and for 180 degrees to either side. Top priority. Sandra?'

He waited until her face replaced Kano's on the tiny screen.

'Correlate all instrument readings for the past month against those presently received. I want detailed comparisons as to temperature and radiation fluctuations. In all future scans include Doppler compensations based on spectrum shift.'

Light had mass, it could be bent by gravitational or magnetic fields, but unless those fields were perfect there would be minor variations. If spotted they could plot the extent of the bubble before them. Light was similar to sound; advancing it rose in pitch, retreating it lowered. A shift to the red meant that a light source was retreating, towards the blue that it was advancing towards them. Again they could only hope for minor alterations, but any information would be of value.

But none would solve the main question.

'What's in there?' Koenig voiced his main worry. 'Victor, what are we heading into?'

'I don't know, John.' Bergman was coldly precise. 'Only time will answer that. But there is another question which should be asked.'

'How can we defend ourselves?' Koenig looked at the other, his face grim. 'I know, Victor. Any suggestions?'

He was aching and sore but alive and all in one piece and, for that, Alan Carter was grateful. Cautiously he stretched, feeling the nag of bruises.

Watching him Helena said, 'Take things easy for a while, Alan. Some heat and massage will help.'

'Ivor?'

He too was all in one piece and still alive but, watching him through the transparent partition, Carter would have wished that, if he had been in the same condition, the instruments registering his physical condition would have dropped to zero. No man, while living, should adopt the appearance of a corpse. No pilot should be staring with dull eyes at the ceiling, his hands limply folded in his lap. No human should lie like a vegetable unable to even smile.

Without turning his head Carter asked, 'How long?'

'Since the trouble.'

'When the Eagle went haywire?'

'There was nothing wrong with the Eagle, Alan. The fault was entirely human. Don't you remember?'

He frowned, remembering only Ivor's sudden madness, his own confusion.

'Paul was monitoring,' she explained. There was no need to lower her voice, Ivor if he could hear would make no response – if he did it would be a step towards recovery, but even so she spoke in a whisper. 'He saw Khokol rise and head for the port and you trying to stop him. There was a struggle and you were thrown to one side. Ivor turned back towards the door but, naturally, Paul had the Eagle on remote control and he couldn't open it. He tried, God how he tried, then, suddenly, he collapsed.'

'And Paul brought us back to Alpha?'

'Yes. You seemed to be unconscious and when you arrived back here—'

'Seemed? I was out, surely.'

'No, Alan.' Helena met his eyes, her own direct. 'You weren't unconscious, not in the way you mean. You were disoriented and on the edge of catatonia, but you weren't asleep or stunned.'

He said, attempting to be casual, 'There's a difference?'

'Medically, yes, but we won't go into that now. It isn't important. I drugged you, gave you hypnotic therapy and some electro-stimulated sleep. Now it's your turn to help me. What happened out there?'

'You know what happened. Ivor went crazy and tried to step out into space. I tried to stop him and got hurt. I guess I was concussed – would that account for it? My condition, I mean?'

He was anxious and Helena could guess why. A pilot had to be fit otherwise he was useless. A man given to psychic breakdown had no place in an Eagle.

'Officially, yes.' Her smile eased his trepidation. 'But there was more to it than that. Did you sense that the Eagle was out of control? Veering? Twisting, perhaps?'

'Yes.'

It had maintained an even course at all times – his own sensory apparatus had been at fault, not the guidance systems of the machine.

'Anything else? Dreams, perhaps? Odd visual effects? Sounds?'

'There was confusion and then darkness. Nothing else.'

'Are you certain?'

He said, stiffly, 'You've known me long enough and well enough to know that I'm not a liar.'

'Alan, I didn't call you that! But I need to know. It's important. Can you remember anything at all after Khokol hit you? I'm not asking you to be factual – we know what happened within the Eagle, but only you can tell us what happened in your mind. You mentioned confusion. Was it visual? Did you hear snatches of song, for example? A voice? Did you experience a sudden, overwhelming desire of some kind? An urge to do something?'

He said, dryly, 'Like opening the port? No. I had no intention of committing suicide.'

'What then?'

For a moment he remained silent and she gained the impression of a man struggling with himself, of overcoming doubts and fears, of surrendering some private citadel.

'Ivor hit me and I fell,' he said, abruptly. 'I was dazed and almost out. The Eagle seemed to be spinning and twisting – you said it wasn't but that's how it felt to me. It grew dark but there were lights and, yes, a voice of some kind. It was like when you are half asleep and barely hear what's going on close at hand. The lights were flashes, dots in the shadows like stars and something moved against them. I was afraid, I think. No, I was afraid and yet at the same time resigned. There was nothing I could do. Then the darkness came and it was like falling into an ebon cloud.' He added, thoughtfully, 'A fall which never seemed to end.'

'The voice – what did it say?'

'I don't know.' He shrugged at her expression. 'I'm not playing games, Doctor, I simply don't know. The words were blurred and almost as if they were foreign. I say "almost" because there was a familiarity about them, but I couldn't make them out.'

'The tone? One of rejection?'

'More of negation.' Carter frowned as he thought about it. 'Someone or something saying a certain thing was not to be. Am I making sense?'

Before answering Helena crossed to her desk and activated an instrument. Carter heard a blur of words, questions and answers, and realised that the present interrogation wasn't the first. He had been questioned under hypnosis; taken from the Eagle, sedated, drugged, cross-examined. His anger died as quickly as it came. To each their responsibility and the burden of that carried by Helena Russell was far from light.

She said, 'Alan, you were very young when your mother died. Correct?'

'Yes.'

'But you remember her.'

'No.'

'You remember her,' she said again. It was not a question. 'A person is a receptive organism and all that happens close at hand is noted and filed within the cortex. Now, those lights, the shape and voice you saw and heard. I suggest that they could have been the reflected illumination of an external source. The shadow that of a woman limned against them. The voice that of your mother telling you to be silent, perhaps. A common occurrence. You agree it might be possible?'

An ancient memory dredged from his subconscious?

'Good,' she said as he nodded. 'As I suspected. It leads to the conclusion that the force responsible is one which triggers various rejective syndromes within the brain. If so it accounts for the diversity of experience common during the warning periods. You were fortunate, Alan.'

'Why?'

'You returned to early childhood. If Paul hadn't withdrawn the Eagle from that sector of space—'

'Back even further?' He had anticipated her reasoning. 'Back to the embryo?'

'Perhaps.'

'Is that what happened to Ivor?'

'No.' Helena glanced to where he lay, eyes open but unseeing. 'He isn't catatonic. Not in the true sense that he has retreated to early childhood to escape the pressures of being an adult and then having to retreat even further because childhood is not a happy time. He has, in a sense, escaped, but in some different form. The fact he tried to open the port worries me. He must have known the danger which means he was subconsciously trying to kill himself.'

'Kill himself? Ivor?'

'He belongs to a race in which the death-wish is very strong.'

Alan glanced at the other, finding it impossible to believe that a man so strong and so fit should be eager to find death. And, if not one, then why not them both? Why had Khokol succumbed and he survived?

‘If all men were alike, Alan,’ said Helena when he put the question, ‘they wouldn’t be men they’d be robots. How do I know? Yet it’s something we’ve got to try and find out and find it soon.’ She glanced at her watch. ‘Within sixty-seven hours to be exact.’

‘Why?’

‘Because that’s when we hit the bubble which almost sent you insane and wrecked Khokol’s mind.’ She looked at where he lay. ‘And what happened to him could happen to us all!’

CHAPTER FOUR

Nothing.

Koenig stared at the screens and felt the tug and pull of frustration. With an effort he kept his face a blank mask, his hands unclenched. To be a commander was more than to give orders. Always he had to present a confident aspect, always to radiate a confidence he might not feel and yet, this time was harder than most.

How to fight an enemy unseen? A danger unknown?

Before him the stars glittered with their usual brightness, the bright expanse of the galaxy glowing as if a rich scatter of gems lay on the sombre velvet of a jeweller's cloth. It was hard to realise that between he and they rested something destructive. A thing which threatened Alpha itself. An invisible killer edging closer even as he watched. A menace which had already caused the death of one man and had reduced another to a mindless shell.

For a moment Koenig had the impression of a crouching beast, alien, horrible, waiting with gaping jaws and venomous sting to grip, to hold, to suck intelligence and life from the hapless prey falling into its grasp.

A moment only, then the illusion was gone and, taking a deep breath, Koenig glanced at the chronometer.

'Minus fifteen seconds, Commander.' Paul spoke from his chair. 'Full strength?'

'Yes.'

'For an indefinite period?' Morrow's voice held doubt. 'The generators might not be able to take maximum load for too long.'

'Full strength for five minutes. Cut for checking then resume for fifteen. Check again then operate at half power until we are an hour from impact.'

An hour from madness and maybe death and the time could be less if the bubble was moving towards them. Bergman doubted that it was. Koenig hoped that he was right.

'Ready to activate,' said Morrow. 'Three, two, one – on!'

A shimmer softened the glow of the stars, a ripple made of broken rainbows which strengthened even as he watched and settled into a sparkling, coruscating bowl which covered the base. Electronic wizardry devised by Bergman and built by the technicians. Forces bent and twisted into channelled lines. Energies formed and held in powerful fields. A defence powered by the strength of the atomic engines, refined in the generators, fed through squat towers and terminals set about the area.

'Loss?'

'Two per cent below normal, Commander.'

'Reason?'

'Maladjustment, I think.' Morrow grunted as he sent his hands flying over his controls. Before him a digital readout moved, figures glowing with ruby flame. 'A slight imbalance, Commander. Now compensated. Operational level one per cent above.'

Under test the screen had withstood the fury of exploding nuclear devices, but what they faced was no familiar form of energy. The screen might be useless and probably was, yet it had to be incorporated into their defences. Koenig glanced again at the chonometer. Two minutes remained of the initial period.

'Boost to absolute maximum, Paul.'

'Commander?'

'Do it!' If the generators were to fail it was better to find out now rather than later. 'Lift and hold.'

The rainbow shimmer thickened, blanked the stars with its coruscating curtain, threw a lamber glow over the Lunar terrain, the surface installations of the base. Distant scanners gave an external view, an inverted bowl dotted with scintillating flashes like tiny explosions; local flares of energy escaping from the confining fields.

'Strength falling,' said Morrow. 'Decay accelerating. Power-loss nine per cent . . . eleven . . . fifteen . . . eighteen . . . Commander?'

'Maintain.' A muscle twitched high on one cheek as Koenig

watched the tell-tales on the consol. Any weakness had to be found and eliminated, suspect points strengthened, extra circuits incorporated if necessary.

'Twenty-one . . . two . . .' Morrow's voice rose and he half turned in his chair. 'A quarter down, Commander!'

'Maintain!'

Hold the torrent of power as the gauges fell and the scintillating flashes grew until they sparkled like a miniature battlefield over the glowing inverted bowl of the dome. Until the meters flashed red and the alarm stabbed the air with its warning snarl.

'Cut!' Koenig drew in his breath as the sound and flashing died. 'Report?'

'Fifty per cent loss of retrieved power – total loss close to seventy-three per cent. Reserve accumulators depleted by a third. Insulation damage on generators two and five. Terminal corrosion on points three to twelve, seventeen to twenty-nine.' Frowning Morrow added, 'I don't understand this. The last regular maintenance report showed all installations at optimum level. Those generators should have stood up better than that.'

'When was the last check made?' Koenig nodded at the answer. 'Before the last warning. I thought so. Can anyone really be certain what they saw and did during that time?'

'Sabotage?' Morrow's voice echoed his incredulity. 'That's tantamount to suicide. Who—' He broke off, remembering, feeling again the terrible revulsion, the urge to run, to hide, to escape. 'Someone maybe tried to kill himself. He rigged the generator in some way hoping it would blow. Maybe, under external stress, it would have blown and taken the entire base with it. If we hadn't tested it as we did – Commander, you could have saved us all!'

A possibility, but the danger was now over. Koenig wondered what had made him abort the original test and push the screen so hard for so long. Instinct, perhaps, the cultivated inner sense which defied all logic and so often provided the right answer.

'Have the engineers check the system,' he ordered. 'All defective parts to be replaced. Summon Professor Bergman to check and test the installation when the work has been completed.' Koenig glanced at the chronometer. 'And tell them to hurry – we have only twelve hours left before impact.'

Helena Russell was asleep and, in her sleep, a man came to her in a dream. He was short, stocky with a neatly trimmed beard and a domed, balding skull. He wore a ceremonial dress coat with a scarlet flower in his lapel and, crossing his torso from his right shoulder to the left hip, a wide ribbon blazed in gold and emerald. She had seen him three times before.

The last had been on the stage of the theatre.

The time before had been when he had given her the highest accolade of her profession short of the Nobel Prize.

The first had been when, as a young student, she had been privileged to attend one of his lectures.

Years ago now, a time when both he and she had been much younger, but always she remembered him as he had been when handing her the award, neatly if fussily dressed in his old-fashioned dress coat, his inevitable flower and the sash which was the decoration he had won from the President of Zaire as a part-reward for saving ten million souls from the ravages of plague.

Professor Emmanual Dylan Batrun.

To her, once, the living symbol of ultimate authority.

And, in the dream, he came to stand before her, moving through wisps of swirling fog, his face blurred a little, his voice distant but as firm and impatient as she remembered.

'In ancient times men thought of a person as consisting of three parts; the brain, the body and the soul. Later, when we, in our arrogance, assumed that only ourselves had been graced with receiving true knowledge, an adjustment was made. The brain became the mind, the body remained and the concept of the soul was medically disposed of. Now a person consisted only of two parts; the body and the mind and it was natural to place them each in their neatly labelled compartments. If the mind was affected then the subject was insane. As insanity has no connection with reality as we have determined what it should be then all statements and utterances of the poor, demented creature could be safely ignored. If the body fell ill then it could be repaired as a mechanic would mend a broken machine. In those enlightened days it was common for eminent surgeons to complain bitterly that, while their operations had been successful, the ungrateful patient had insisted on dying.'

A calculated pause; time in which to take a sip of water, to adjust his flower, to move a little to ease incipient cramp, to allow the sychophantic laughter to fade into a respectful silence.

In her dream Helena saw it all as she had seen it before. Turning she looked at an endless expanse of barren desert, sere beneath a lambent sun, the grit strewn with a stark litter of bone; fleshless skulls watching her with cavernous sockets, teeth bared in the parody of a smile.

On the podium the archaic figure continued as before.

'. . . is a tedious thing. It is hard to accept the fact that we may have been wrong and it is easy to look for simple answers to involved questions. A sane man becomes deranged – how convenient to say that a demon has possessed him. A man's body is not as it should be – obviously the humours are not working in true harmony. Words!' The dry voice held the crack of a whip. 'Rubbish! What is a demon? What are humours? Define! Define before you can hope to understand!'

The figure blurred, wavered, mist rising to stream in wreaths and tendrils of luminous colour. A rainbow swirled and, for a moment, she was conscious of an aching poignancy. So dear the departed days! So sweet the illusions of youth! So rich the future which had yet to come!

'Doctor! Doctor Russell!'

Mathias was beside her, his face reflecting his concern. As she opened her eyes he lifted his hand from her shoulder.

'Bob?'

'You were restless,' he said. 'Crying out.'

'A dream,' she said. 'I was young again and listening to Professor Batrun. In Vienna at the Institute. He was talking of the interaction of body and mind.' With a smooth motion she sat upright and clasped her hands around her lifted knees. 'A great man, Bob. A great physician and a wonderful psychiatrist. I think it was he who guided me to take an interest in space medicine. Something he said – I can't remember just what, but a hint, maybe, a little verbal push.'

'A psychological nudge.' He nodded, understanding. 'Something similar happened to me. Coffee?'

'Please.'

She watched as he went to get it, looking around at the empty ward. She had rested for a moment on one of the beds, intending only to relax for a moment, to ease the tension of mind and body, and had obviously fallen asleep. She stretched, feeling the tug of her uniform, noting the blanket which lay to one side. Mathias had covered her, had looked in from time to time and, in the last, had touched her gently to reassure her, to offer what comfort his presence could provide.

She smiled as he returned with steaming cups of coffee.

'Thank you, Bob. Did you ever meet the professor?'

'No. He had retired by the time I graduated and was dead before I'd gained my doctorate.'

A few years, she thought, suddenly reminded of the age differential between them. Less than a decade but it had robbed him of the chance of meeting a genius.

She sipped her coffee, grateful for its warmth and comfort, mulling the accomplishments of the dead. Batrun had been a rebel, tearing down accepted beliefs, hurling challenges at the establishment, mocking ancient traditions. For years he had wandered in the wilderness, damned by his unorthodox experiments in mind-body function. An accident had saved him. The daughter of the President of some South American Republic had crashed to wander in the jungle. Saved she had been insane. Taken to Batrun she had been cured.

Then had come the disaster at Zaire.

'He was lucky,' said Mathias as if he had been reading her thoughts. 'The chance of being in the right place at the right time.'

'But he proved his contention.'

'And again was fortunate. The girl could have died or remained permanently insane.' Mathias took a sip of coffee. 'I wonder why you dreamed of him?'

A subconscious association, of course, but exactly what?

Sitting on the bed, knees uplifted, sipping her coffee Helena thought about it. The lecture itself was nothing; a replayed mental recording. It had only repeated elemental facts, now common knowledge, of the association between mental and physical health, the basic unity of both and the influence of external sensory stimuli to each individual picture of reality. Touch a man with a red-hot poker after mentally convincing him that he is to be touched by ice and he will not blister or suffer hurt. Conversely, once convinced that a feather is a sword, and flesh will part, wounds bleed and bones break beneath its impact.

'*Define!*' Batrun had said. '*Define before you can hope to understand!*'

Define what?

The present problem?

What else had she been trying to do!

'Doctor?' Mathias had seen the sudden tension of her hand, the betrayed emotion. 'Is something wrong?'

'I'm a fool, Bob, that's what is wrong. We've been trying to find out what happened during the warnings and what happened to Alan and Ivor Khokol out there in space. We've been hoping to find a shield of some kind to protect us.'

'So?'

'A wrong definition. We don't have to beat the situation, just find a way to live with it. We know, for example, that some force is inducing mental derangement by some form of cortical stimulus. We can't prevent it as yet but perhaps we can negate its effects in some way.'

'With drugs?'

'If possible.' She set aside the coffee. 'Can you think of anything which would do?'

'We have quite a selection,' he said. 'Alcohol, for example, the ancient anesthetic. It is a depressant and throws the motor systems all to hell if enough is taken. It confuses the reality-sense and could work if the application and control could be maintained. Unfortunately there are unpredictable side-effects which makes its use undesirable. Tranquilisers?'

'Numb emotional reaction but we want more than a delayed

reaction.' Helena rose and inflated her lungs, her figure sharply prominent against the taut material of her uniform. 'As I see it the thing is to affect the synapses in some way. If mentally received stimuli can be prevented from conversion into physical activity then we will have found some form of defence. Acetycholine, perhaps?'

'It could hold the answer,' admitted Mathias. 'We know it is an essential ingredient in the passing on of nerve impulses. We can destroy it with the enzyme cholinesterase so if we could compound something combining a form of paralytic agent coupled with a reality-distorter such as LSD – no, Doctor. There would be no way to predict the action of such a hell's brew.'

'But we must try, Bob,' said Helena. 'We must try.'

'Nothing.' Sandra Benes looked up from her instruments. 'Space ahead is still apparently clear. All receptors negative.'

'Incredible!' Bergman narrowed his eyes, heavy lines creasing his cheeks. 'I would have sworn that, so close to the impact-point, some aberration would have been obvious. No trace of any stellar displacement on the comparison-runs?'

'None.'

'Nor temperature differentials?' Bergman grunted at her negative shake of the head. 'Well, John, that leaves us with nothing but speculation and intelligent assumptions.'

'Such as?'

'The warning field could either be of great depth and some distance from the actual area or the forces which rotate the electro-magnetic spectrum are of an immensely high order. In that case...'

He rambled on but Koenig wasn't paying full attention. Instead he moved to where the internal monitors scanned the interior of the base, running his eyes over the screens, noting small points and sensing again the unusual eeriness of what he saw. Always, when the base was on red alert, there was an unusual and intangible atmosphere. A silence, a tension as of a coiled spring, an awareness which held something of the animal poised to strike, but now there was an added quality.

The guards were in their places, the technicians at their posts, all security areas sealed. But now those doors had been welded shut, the passages were deserted, all non-essential personnel confined to their quarters. On the screens the rooms and corridors were deserted and, to Koenig, Alpha gained the appearance of a ghost town, an empty village, a sepulchre.

A bad thought and one he dismissed with an irritable shake of the head. Alpha was far from dead. It was a citadel prepared for the unknown. Once the warning barrier had been passed – what?

From his consol Paul Morrow said, quietly, 'Twenty-five minutes to go, Commander.'

'The defences?'

'At optimum.' Morrow glanced at the screens showing the coruscating bowl of protective energy which covered the base. 'Ten per cent more available power for emergency boost if required.'

'Save it until moment of impact. Set up an automatic switch to throw in all power one minute before contact and to maintain it for – how long can the installation take boosted power, Victor?'

'On emergency overload about thirty minutes.'

'For twenty-five minutes, Paul.' It should be long enough, if not a few minutes would serve no purpose, but to burn out the installation would leave them defenceless against normal dangers.

Helena had done her best to provide a safeguard against the rest.

Koenig looked at the capsule she placed in his hand. It was large, smooth, brightly coloured and he was reminded of a sugared almond, but the hard outer coating held not a nut but a chemical combination of involved complexity. He watched as she handed one to everyone in Main Mission.

As she returned to face him he said, 'What is it, Helena'

'A witch's brew.' She shrugged at his expression. 'Guesswork mostly, we've had no time to make thorough tests, but it should help. Think of it as water which will damp down a fire. If things get too bad bite down on the coating, break it, the liquid inside will be absorbed by the inner membranes and enter the bloodstream. As I said it should act like a deluge of water on a flame.'

Looking at his own capsule Bergman said, 'My guess is that it contains an anti-hallucinogenic coupled with a strong tranquiliser and maybe a curare derative. Am I right?'

'As much as you'd be right if you said that a house consisted of bricks, planks and plaster. Don't worry about what's in it, just take it if you feel that you are losing control. You too, John.'

'Yes, Helena.'

'I mean it.' She looked at his face, the curve of his eyebrows, the set of his jaw. A face which revealed his inner strength and determination. One she didn't want to see turned into a slack, idiotic mask as Ivor Khokol's had been. The man who now lay like a vegetable in Medical. 'Take care, John.'

'You too, Helena.'

Her duties were with the sick, her place in the Section she commanded, and he watched her go, turning back to the screens only after the doors had closed behind her.

'Nine,' said Morrow. 'Nine minutes to go.'

'Sandra?'

'Still nothing, Commander.'

Nothing to do but wait as the seconds dragged past, as the hands of the chronometer swept around and around the illuminated dial, as the digital counters flipped to show a reducing number of figures. Minutes and seconds pouring through the sieve of time.

'Five seconds,' breathed Bergman. 'Three . . . two . . . one . . .'

Madness!

CHAPTER FIVE

It came in a wave, a flood, a crashing deluge which tore at the fabric of reality and turned the familiar into the strange. The lights changed, the instruments became grimacing faces, the floor a stinking morass which sucked at the feet with liquid squelchings. And, abruptly, each was alone.

David Kano sucked in his breath, feeling the fear of dreadful knowledge, the soul-twisting terror which urged him to run before it was too late. They were coming for him, he knew it, the tall and dreadful shapes with their painted masks and skirts of grass, their bells and clawed sticks, the instruments of pain and torment. The forest rustled with them, the firelight limned their figures, the ghost-masks, the devil-masks, the depicted god-faces.

Men seeking to kill.

Men hating him for what he was and what he had.

Animals which would take him and send his spirit shrieking from his flesh to linger in an everlasting agony.

He crouched, trembling, the beat of drums matching the pounding of his heart. He could smell the stink of his own sweat redolent of his own fear. Beneath his naked feet the mud sucked at him like a living thing.

Behind him Computer reared to the sky.

Computer – his God.

He straightened and the drums became a rolling sussuration, the leaping torchlight a ruby illumination painting the faces before him; rapt faces alive with awe and respect. Those who had come to kneel and worship at the base of the god and its priest. The god Computer and the priest Kano.

Kano the priest. He Who Learned. He Who Knew All Answers. He Who Served.

Turning he lifted his arms towards the rearing bulk of the god-machine. Behind him the worshippers sucked in their breaths and the drums, more sonorous now, rolling with a relentless deliberation, boomed like distant thunder.

Computer was god. Computer knew all things. Computer was all-powerful. Great was Computer's priest. Great was Kano.

'Kano!' The shout lifted towards the stars. 'Kano! Kano! Kano!'

The clash of spears and the throbbing of tribal drums, the racial memory of long-lost days, oiled bodies like ebon in the torchlight, paint, masks, blood – one who challenged.

'Kano!'

The law of the jungle – kill or die!

'Kano!'

An image of himself, tall, oiled, naked aside from paint, hands tipped with claws which reached to rip and tear. His own hands reaching in turn, gripping, holding, his jaws open to bite.

Teeth closing to crunch on something brittle.

Darkness!

In Medical something stirred. A man who had turned into a vegetable and who now became a man again. Ivor Khokol sighed and lifted an arm and sat upright holding the reins of his horse, feeling the pound of its hooves as it carried him towards glory.

He had slept, he thought, dozing in the saddle, an old trick of the Hiung when engaged on a long journey. Now he turned to look at the massed riders behind, a loose column which stretched back to the horizon. They were heading south, to Rome, to the loot of the ancient world.

To the woman of his dreams.

She was tall and blonde and he had seen her face limned against the stars. From her he would gain fine sons, men-children who would grow into warriors and be an added strength to his arm. Once he had been afraid of her, of the power she held, but that time was over and now she would crumple in his hands.

'On!' He yelled. 'On!'

Helena heard the cry.

She sat at her desk, motionless, even her eyes unshifting in their sockets. In her bloodstream flowed a complicated mass of chemicals, a stronger combination than what she had given to the others, one whose efficiency she was now testing.

From an instrument before her a light winked at one-second intervals. Reality.

With the light came a high-pitched bleep. Reality.

Two checks at least – if she could remember them. Two anchors to a familiar world. A pair of signposts which would remain unaffected by whatever mental storm might overwhelm her.

Now she stared at a light which burned continuously, heard a sound without break.

Like worms her thoughts crawled to match the observed phenomena.

'. . . time sense affected . . . disorientation of associated stimuli . . . no sense of physical contact with chair or desk . . . vision affected . . . bodily temperature seems higher than normal . . . metabolic change . . . hearing . . .'

'On!' A harsh yell, repeated 'On!'

Ivor Khokol riding with his warriors to the sack of Rome.

He came running from the place in which she had left him to halt, staring, hands moving before him as if they held reins, body twitching to the motions of an invisible mount. Like a child riding a hobby-horse, she thought, and resisted the impulse to laugh.

What an amusing hallucination!

In turn he saw a shimmer of gold.

Rome!

In Rome was all the gold of the world and now it was before him, lambent in the glowing sun, rich, inviting, waiting for him to touch it, to scoop it into his arms. Dismounting he ran towards it, seeing it change to become a piled mass of delicate strands.

A change which left him unmystified – all men knew of the magic owned by the ancient keepers of hallowed temples. And gold was gold no matter in what form it came.

Helena rose as he came forward, feeling her fragile defences begin to crack, the chemical walls splinter so that the world dissolved into a shower of shattered gems which filled the air with a smoking, scintillating kaleidoscope. Shapes became distorted, the desk turned into a crouching, snarling beast carved from obsidian, the walls vanished to be replaced by an endless vista of rolling plains, the roof became an emerald sky.

Khokol became a nightmare.

She backed from the squat, hairy, snarling thing which came towards her, hopping like a toad, webbed hands extended, bulging eyes glowing with a killer's rage. Her back hit something solid and she turned and saw a row of jars each containing a severed human head. Eyes watched her, unblinking, the whites of the balls veined with a tracery of red.

On them spiders fed.

'No!' The sight was vile. Disgusting. 'No!'

A hand clawed at her side, ripped at her uniform, fingers touching her bared skin. A foetid odour stung her nostrils and slime spattered her hair. Weight pulled at her, threw her to the ground, sent her sprawling, looking into the ridged and mottled face of a repulsive monstrosity.

'No!'

Pressure flattened her hips, forced apart her thighs, held her shoulders hard against the floor. The stench of rotting teeth filled her nostrils, the odour of suppuration and gangrene wafted about her, slime touched her, filth embraced her.

'No!'

Once, ages ago, she had been attacked by crazed degenerates while working in a hospital. They had intended rape and murder. She had escaped then and hard-won experience came to her aid now. A scream followed the upward jerk of a knee. Another the stabbing action of her thumbs. A third, followed by a liquid gurgle, the savage chop of her stiffened hand.

The weight holding her fell away and she rose to run, to stand, to gasp while the universe spun around her.

The anchors!

Where were her anchors?

The light and the sound. The desk on which the instrument

sat. The drugs which lay beneath housed in their air-powered hypodermic. Release from the nightmare which held her, the madness in which she was lost.

Moving she tripped and fell to rise sobbing, hands extended, groping as if blind. A flash and a high, thin note. A flash, a sound, another flash. An eye winking . . . winking . . . winking . . .

Something like a dagger which hissed as she thrust it against her throat.

Koenig stirred, feeling the hardness beneath his cheek, the wetness on face and chin. There was a bitter, acrid taste in his mouth together with something sharp and jagged. He spat it out, stirred sat upright, his head swimming with a momentary nausea. Touching his chin he found it thick with blood.

It had come from his nose and from a minor gash on his tongue; the result of the sharp coating of the capsule he had crushed beneath his teeth when, at the end, the battle for his sanity had been lost.

Sitting, eyes closed, head lowered to rest on his knees, he saw again the parade of nightmare.

The base a wreck, rooms shattered, panels splintered, the screens ripped free and hanging blind and dead. As the personnel lay broken and lifeless all around. Like a bereft ghost he had wandered through Alpha, seeing nothing but desolation, unable to understand why he alone had remained alive.

Pictures remained; Paul lying with his spine broken, one hand twitching, blood streaming from his parted lips. Kano, face distorted with the rictus of death, arms clutched around his precious machine. Victor, his stomach spilling intestines, skull pulped, one eyeball resting on his cheek. Helena—

He didn't want to remember how she had appeared.

How she could still appear.

'No!'

He was dead and damned, alone in the ruin of his command, all he had ever held precious gone for all time, ruined, thrown away by his stubborn refusal to retreat, to withdraw, to return. The tears had stung his eyes even as he had fought the sickness mounting within him. Empty rooms and compartments, living quarters looking like a shambles, red against the white, red against the green, red against blue and yellow and orange. Red, red everywhere, a deluge of blood.

'No!' Even in memory it was too much and he shivered, fighting the sickness, feeling again the rage which had joined it, the killing fury against whoever or whatever had done this thing to him and to his people. 'No!'

The windows had been shattered, the air gone, but he was still alive. The power had failed and shadows had accentuated the horror, grim shapes limned by the pale glow of the emergencies, yet he could feel the beat of light against his lids. He had been hurt, dying, yet the wetness was only that of sweat and a little blood.

Koenig opened his eyes.

Bergman stared at him, his skull intact, both eyes in place, forehead bearing a familiar crease.

'John!' he said. 'John! Thank God!'

Koenig rose. At his consol Paul Morrow was shaking his head even as his fingers danced over his controls. Kano, looking a peculiar shade of grey beneath his brown skin, was at his position. His eyes were bloodshot and scratches marked his cheeks but his lips were free of the ugly smile Koenig remembered.

'Commander!' Sandra Benes, pale, fragile, looked like delicate porcelain. 'You're all right. I thought – thank God you're all right!'

'Paul?'

'It's over,' said Bergman before Morrow could answer. 'We've passed through whatever it was caused those hallucinations. Helena's drug helped us. Without it I doubt if we could have survived. Even as it was it – well, never mind. John?'

'I'm all right.' Koenig wiped at his face then rubbed his smeared hand against his uniform. He was still a little dazed, still unable to fully grasp that the death and devastation he had seen had only been a nightmare. An illusion. Something born of fear and the disorientation of his sensory apparatus. And something of the horror remained. 'Helena!'

'She's all right, John.' Bergman was quick with his reassurance. 'Paul has checked out Medical.'

'I must talk to her.' His fingers were trembling too much and the commlock fell as he snatched it from his belt. 'Get her on screen. Get her!'

A moment and it was done and Koenig felt a sudden relaxation as he looked at the pale face framed by the mass of golden hair. Not dead, then. Not torn and ravaged, ripped and abused, left like a foul obscenity on the sterile floor. Not a ghastly travesty of the human form left in careful array; the art-form of a diseased and degenerate beast.

'John?' Her eyes widened as she searched his face. 'John – what is wrong?'

'Nothing. Are you all right?'

'Yes, but—'

'Get up here.' Duty overrode inclination, the need to have her close, to reassure himself that what he had seen had truly been an hallucination. 'Wait. Can Bob manage? He can? Good, then join me at once.'

'But, John, I must—'

'Join me!'

As he blanked the screen Morrow said, 'I can tell you what she wanted to report, Commander. Ivor Khokol went crazy and tried to kill her. She had to defend herself.'

'And?' Had the attack been the cause of his nightmare? Her fear somehow transmitted to his fevered brain? Sadistic images born of fear or received from her attacker? 'And what, Paul? Answer me!'

'He was dead when they found him.'

Killed without intent, a victim of the general distortion – and how many others would have died had they not been locked away and safely drugged? Koenig drew in his breath and shook his head. He still felt dazed, divorced from his surroundings, and he guessed that he had crushed the capsule later than he should have done. The others had obviously recovered before him and appeared to be showing less of the effects of the mind-distorting field through which they had passed.

'Here, John. It may help.'

Silently he took the container of water Bergman handed to him, swallowing the pills which accompanied it, washing them down together with the acrid taste of chemicals and blood.

Helena appeared as the drug began to take effect. Quickly she examined his face, wiped away the blood and gave a tremulous smile.

'John, I must tell you. Something dreadful happened and—'

'I know. Paul told me.' He stared at her, devouring her with his eyes. Tall, whole, clean, unhurt – thank God it had only been an illusion!

'Base intact, no damage, all systems operational,' reported Morrow from his consol. 'One dead three with minor injuries – all self-inflicted. Defence screens at optimum.'

And nothing lay before them.

Koenig stared at the screens, seeing only what had been visible before, the cold glitter of distant stars, the fuzz of distant nebulae. They had passed through hell and arrived – where?

'Sandra?'

'Nothing, Commander. All – no, wait! I am receiving positive indications of a strong force-emission lying directly ahead. Magnetic field of incredible density.' She gave the figures and Bergman shook his head.

'Amazing! Such firm control! Do you realise what this means, John? A near-total restraining of all leakage. Obviously the outer barrier through which we have passed utilised any seepage of energy to power the psychic force-field which serves as a warning and defence. How far, Sandra?'

'Close.' She looked up, her face strained. 'We should reach it within two minutes.'

'Full boost on defensive shield!' snapped Koenig. 'Sound the red alert. Activate all external scanners.'

He felt Helena at his side and took her hand in his own, his fingers firm against the warmth of her skin. He caught the scent of her perfume, a delicate floral aroma, and a strand of her golden hair caressed his cheek.

'The transition point,' murmured Bergman. 'This is where all light and radiation is seized by the enveloping forces and rotated in a half-circle. If we were a photon of light or even a minute particle of spacial debris we too could be so rotated.

'But the Moon had tremendous mass and any force which could move it so quickly from its destined path would volatise the entire body to incandescent vapour.'

'John!' whispered Helena. 'John, I—'

'Now!'

The screens blurred as Bergman called out, stars seeming to flow from the centre to the edges, to wink, to vanish . . .

To be replaced by a wall of utter darkness.

A blank, ebon surface which served as a backdrop to something incredible.

'John!' Helena's fingers dug into his hand, the nails gouging at his flesh. 'John – it's a brain! A living, human brain!'

CHAPTER SIX

It shone with a pulsating greenish glow, a leprous luminescence blotched with the lines of convolutions, divided into sponge-like hemispheres, rounded and soft-looking and incredible.

'A brain!' Bergman's voice reflected his amazement. 'But big! So big!'

The size of the Moon as seen from Earth, tremendous, dominating. Koenig stared at it, noting details unseen before, the haze-like appearance of the thing, the blurred detail, the pulse of the greenish glow. The image blurred even more as he watched.

'Paul?'

'Interference, Commander. The external scanners are being affected by the discharge from our defensive shield.' His voice rose a little, 'Discharge far higher than normal. A radiated loss of seven per cent and mounting.'

Koenig moved his eyes and stared at the external view of the screen. The surface was glowing, bright with emitted energy, scintillating with eye-hurting brilliance.

'Sandra – any sign of anything approaching?'

'No, Commander.'

'No attacking vessels, then, and it would do no harm to drop the shield.' The image in the main screens cleared as Morrow collapsed the shield, sharpening in detail, shining with an inner light, an emerald mystery.

It couldn't be a brain. Not a human, pulsating, living organ – the size alone was against it being that. Koenig listened as Sandra Benes reported the findings of her instruments.

'Mass 2.365 Lunar. Volume 5.463. Distance .025 au. Local radiation 7.973 plus normal. Temperature—' She broke off then said, unsteadily, 'Apparently zero.'

'Check!'

'I've done that, Commander. Our instruments must be defective in some way. No light-source can have zero temperature and yet that is what we appear to be looking at.'

A mystery, another to add to the rest, but the solutions could wait. Koenig's first responsibility was to the base and he listened as the reports came in.

'All systems operating. No damage. Alpha at optimum.' Morrow turned in his chair. 'Stand down from red alert, Commander?'

'Yes. Switch to yellow. What do you make of it, Victor?'

Bergman was already at work with his circular slide rules, his computer terminal and other apparatus.

'A moment, John. Kano, will you please check this analogue with computer? Thank you.' He pursed his lips as the technician handed him the readout. 'As I suspected. Interesting. Most interesting.'

Koenig said, tightly, 'No games, Victor. I want answers.

'We have passed through the outer wall of force isolating this area from the normal universe. Naturally the parameters are dark because no light is being received – all is being rotated around the circumference of this space. We are, fortunately, travelling on a line which will bisect the sphere on a chord towards its lower region. I say "fortunately" because if we had been travelling in a more direct line towards the centre then a collision with the central mass would have been inevitable.' Bergman made an adjustment on his rule and frowned at the result. 'At our velocity and knowing the relative masses of the two bodies both would have been totally shattered.'

The death and devastation the warning had meant?

'And?'

'Be a little patient, John. We have, in effect, entered a completely new universe and it will take a little time to learn something about it. After all we have taken two million years to learn about our own and still are ignorant.'

'Please, Victor, no lectures. Can you anticipate any immediate danger?'

'Immediate? No.'

'Conclusions?'

Bergman sighed and shook his head. 'You ask a hard question, John, and I can only give the roughest of answers. Basically we should, if conditions are as we know, merely proceed until eventually we will leave this area as we entered it. Imagine a circle. Imagine an object, the tip of a pen, for example. It moves on a straight line, hits one side of the circle, passes on, crosses the area and leaves the ring on the far side. We are the tip of the pen and this space is the circle.'

One containing the tremendous representation of a human brain. Koenig glanced at it where it hung in the screens, grotesque, monstrous, and knew himself to be the victim of suggestion and illusion.

The thing could not be a human brain.

It couldn't be a brain at all.

The colour was wrong, a brain would have been grey and streaked with red, not a pulsating green. Helena had planted the suggestion, forming an association with a familiar object, turning a vague similarity into a firm depiction. The dark lines of assumed convolutions must be fissures and valleys, the green that of vegetation, the apparent pulsation a fault in the scanners, the glow—?

'Sandra – still no temperature?'

'None that we are registering, Commander.'

Cold light? It was possible – some insects had the facility of producing a glow by chemical means, but Koenig knew that nothing radiating that brightly could possibly do it without emitting energy of some kind. And that energy would register as heat.

'Check on the complete electro-magnetic spectrum. Kano, feed all received data into computer for the purpose of constructing a local analogue of our present and extrapolated situation. Anything new as yet, Paul?'

'Findings are being correlated, Commander.' Morrow grew busy with his instruments. 'Additional data on screens now.' The image of the glowing central mass shifted and something else took its place. 'This was behind the main body and has just come into view.'

It was a ball of something which could have been rock but the surface was rounded, smooth, a dull grey illuminated by the green glow and resembling a polished pebble. A natural satellite of the central mass, perhaps, but Koenig didn't think so.

Bergman had no alternative answer.

'It could have been trapped sometime in the past. Given enough time other objects beside ourselves must have entered this pocket universe. That could have been a lump of stellar debris at one time, a small planetoid or a large meteor.'

'Trapped,' said Koenig. 'How? Why? If it entered then why didn't it leave?'

'There could be many reason,' said Bergman, precisely. 'It could have had a low relative velocity. It could have bisected this space very near the central mass and have been caught by its gravitational attraction. Or—'

Koenig snapped, 'Kano! Have computer check on those possibilities.'

'John?' Bergman frowned. 'Is something on your mind?'

'Never take the obvious for granted, Victor. You were one of the first to teach me that. Just because an answer appears to be the logical solution doesn't mean that it is correct. Kano?'

'The possibilities mentioned by Professor Bergman are mutually conflicting.' David Kano cleared his throat as he studied the readout. 'Assuming the relative masses to be the same as at present observed the difference in relative velocity would have had to be small for the intruder to be trapped into a stable orbit. But if it had been so low then it would have been drawn by gravitational attraction into the main body.'

'In other words,' said Koenig, grimly, 'If the intruder was moving slow enough to be trapped then it wouldn't have been moving fast enough to avoid destruction. So much for logical answers, Victor. Want to try again?'

Bergman said, slowly, 'There's another answer, but we don't know enough yet about local conditions to be sure if it is correct. I hope that it isn't.'

'Why?'

'This could be a closed-system, John. A miniature universe with his own laws and own energy-levels which have little relation to those with which we are familiar. In that case—' He paused then said, bleakly, 'It could be that everything entering this space is trapped. We could go on and on but all we'd be doing is to follow the interior of this space around and around. If that is the case then we are caught – trapped for eternity!'

Bob Mathias adjusted the microscope, stared through the eyepiece, made a further adjustment and, after another examination, leaned back from the instrument. He was frowning, twin lines graven deep between his eyes, the corners of his mouth downturned a little as if he had looked at something unpleasant.

'Doctor?' Nurse Sinto halted at his side. She was trim and neat in her uniform, olive skin enhanced by the stark whiteness of her sleeve. 'You look perturbed, is something wrong?'

'I'm not sure.'

'Not to be sure is to be aware of life,' she smiled. 'Only the dead can be certain of the absence of change.'

'Which is an apparent contradiction as you know. If dead there can be no certainty.'

'True,' admitted the girl. 'And with only one hand how can there be clapping?'

Mathias shook his head. At times he found the girl impossible. Young, attractive, Avril Sinto seemed to take a delight in firing abstruse quotations at him, many of which he was fairly certain she invented on the spot, but she was, he had to admit, a superb master of her trade and for that he could tolerate much.

And he liked her. Liked her, perhaps, a little too much.

'Avril—'

'Bob?' He had broken the coldly formal manner of professional address and she reminded him of it with the use of his given name and a smile. 'Were you going to invite me to join you after duty? I've a recording of Gus Halliday's *Lunar Approach*, remember it? The one with the simulated rocket blast and the sub-audible voices? If you want you could come to my quarters and listen to it.'

'Thank you, Avril, but no.'

'Don't you like good music?'

'Good music, yes.' He softened his rejection. 'You know the wise old saying? One man's meat is another's poison? Gus Halliday may be a good musician to you but to me he's a—'

'Careful, Bob!' she warned with mock ferocity. 'You're talking of the man I could have loved. But I know what you mean. To be honest I borrowed the recording because I thought you might like it. Now I've found we have yet another thing in common. Well, what else can we do? I know! Take me to the observation room. I've heard the view now is fantastic. Is it true that Doctor Russell first described the central body as a brain?'

'I don't know. I wasn't in Main Mission at the time.'

'Well, it is. Nurse Tyde told me. She's seen it. A brain, Bob. Think of it. A planet-sized brain.'

'Or something which just happens to resemble one,' he corrected. 'A walnut looks the same only much smaller. That's why the Romans used to think it good for headaches and such. The similarity of appearance made them think the two were connected in some way.' He sighed, wistfully, 'Medicine in those days was simple.'

'Hit and miss, Bob. If it worked you did it again. Now we know exactly what we're doing and why.'

'Do we?' His shrug was expressive. 'I wish I could be as sure.'

She caught his tone, recognising its seriousness, and immediately became the true professional she was. The time for informality had passed.

'There is something wrong! What is it, Doctor?'

'I'm not sure. Perhaps nothing more than a contaminated culture. I've been checking blood corpuscles and noted something strange. Then I checked out a culture of bacteria, X238 – a harmless but essential component of the lower bowel.'

'And?'

'Probably nothing. It could even be fatigue. In any case I'll have to check again. If you could prepare two cultures for me, nurse?'

'X238?'

'Yes.'

'Both on agar?'

She moved away as he nodded and, alone, he turned again to the microscope. Lost in the magnified world of sub-cultures he didn't hear Helena approach him. Only when she rested her hand on his shoulder did he lift his head.

'What? Oh, Doctor Russell!'

'Did I startle you?'

'No – I wasn't expecting you. How is Shaw?'

'He'll be all right.' Shaw was one of those who had recently injured himsef. 'Some superficial bruising, minor contusions but the fractured ribs we suspected turned out to be little more than hair-line breaks.' Helena glanced at the notes Mathias had made. 'Blood-checks, Bob?'

'A routine count. I'm a little concerned about Ellman. He isn't recovering as he should and I suspect a lowered red-cell count.'

'Ellman?' Helena frowned. 'He was discharged as fit before we hit the barrier. Before—' She swallowed then forced herself to continue, 'Before Ivor Khokol collapsed.'

'Yes.' Mathias removed the slide from the instrument and selected another. 'You remember how concerned we were at Sam Blake's prolonged hospitalisation. His wound seemed reluctant to heal. Well, I've been doing some research on the problem, no answer as yet and maybe there never will be, but I did bump into something odd when I tested out Ellman's blood. He was injured about the same time and suffered the same superficial conditions. Well – look at this.'

He stepped aside as Helena stooped over the microscope. For a long moment she examined the slide.

'And?'

'Now examine this.'

'A comparison?'

She turned at his nod and again became engrossed in her study of the illuminated picture beneath the lenses. Without speaking she selected other slides then looked at his notes.

'You made other tests, Bob?'

'On X238 – they check out.' He drew in his breath and held it for a moment before releasing it in an audible sigh. 'I'm having fresh cultures made, of course, but I'm afraid the picture is clear.'

Helena looked at him; a skilled man, an experienced physician and a master of pathology. Not a man to be easily terrified and not one to show unfounded anxiety. And far too good a scientist to leap to unfounded assumptions.

Yet she had to know. Gently she said, 'You suspect disease, Bob?'

'You saw.'

'I saw, yes, but I want you to say it. You have done the tests and made the conclusions. I ask you again, Bob. Disease?'

'No,' he said. 'Age.'

The observation room was fitted with chairs and soft coverings with a fountain giving musical tinklings; a susurration of subdued melody designed to give the impression of warmth and security, the balmy magic of a summer's evening, a scented, sub-tropical night.

Here lovers came to walk beneath the stars, to sit and whisper sweet promises. Here too came the tired and those who felt the need to stretch the vision into the infinite. And, here, too, came artists and poets seeking inspiration, those who felt the need to be alone, others who wished to cherish memories of a vanished age.

From a shadowed place against one curved wall Koenig looked at dimly seen heads, saw the glimpses of arms and legs, the pale blur of lifted faces, other faces, darker, gleaming like ebony, like sun-kissed fruit. If any saw him they gave no sign and he, in turn, stood as if he were a man in total isolation.

That, too, was an attribute of the room. In it, should that be the desire, privacy was absolute.

A privacy now invaded by the watchful eye of the alien sun.

Words, he thought, ones which had little meaning and which, even so, were wrong. The thing was not a sun and it was far from alien. Here, in this place, it belonged and Alpha did not. The Moon was the intruder. They were the alien interlopers.

And they would remain alien – for how long?

Again Koenig stared at the enigmatic, brain-like core of the central mass. Its greenish radiation pulsed as if in response to the pound of a living heart. Its shape, all the more disquieting because of medical associations, gave it the appearance of a monstrosity. Its satellite, unseen now, had vanished behind the main body which hung low above the horizon. An accident had made it so – had they entered the mysterious area at a slightly different angle then it would have appeared directly overhead.

Lifting the commlock from his belt Koenig triggered the instrument and read the digital time-check thrown on the tiny screen.

It vanished as he pressed a stud.

'Victor?'

'John!' Bergman was in his private laboratory, seated, a litter of graphs and paper before him. 'Where are you?' He nodded as Koenig answered. 'Waiting?'

'Yes. How much longer?'

'Without precise measurements we have to allow for a wide margin of error. And, as you know, we had trouble in determining the area of this space. Even now we have only a rough approximation.'

'How long?'

'You'll know as soon as we find out, John. Don't ask for the impossible.'

A stubborn man, thought Koenig as the screen went blank. But a less stubborn one would have been dead long ago and, certainly, without that trait Bergman would never have achieved his fame. For that, if nothing else, he should be respected.

But it was hard to wait.

Hard to hang on the edge of a precipice of doubt, not knowing if a simple matter of time would solve their problem by showing there was no problem at all, or whether the hopes and entire life-style of the base would have to be changed.

For, if they were trapped, change would be inevitable.

The commlock hummed and he looked at Sandra's smooth and lovely face.

'Commander! We have determined—'

'Wait! I'm coming to join you. Have Professor Bergman notified.'

He was already in Main Mission when Koenig arrived, standing to one side of the consol, his face heavy with deeply graven lines. An expression which told Koenig the worst.

'We're trapped?'

'I – yes, John. I'm afraid so.'

'Kano?'

'Computer verifies, Commander. Our measured distance from the central body is remaining static. Sufficient time has lapsed for our velocity to have carried us away from it if we were continuing to move in a straight line relative to this area.'

'But how?' Koenig frowned as he snapped the question. 'Our relative mass is too great for us to have been caught by gravitational attraction. And our velocity was too high for us to be swung into orbit so soon.'

'In our own universe you would be right,' said Bergman. 'But, as I warned, the rules here are not the same as those outside. Direction, velocity, mass – all have different meanings. And there's something more. Sandra?'

'All surface instrument readings are betraying an extremely odd condition, Commander. There is an increasing amount of energy potential radiating from the Moon and apparently streaming into space.'

'What?' Koenig glared his incredulity. 'Energy *leaving* the surface?'

'Yes.'

'That doesn't make sense. We should be receiving it from the sun – the main body. It's radiating light and there must be other energy-emissions. Yet you say – Paul?'

'Monitors, confirm, Commander. The base is suffering a continual energy-loss.'

'Scale?'

'Treble normal and mounting.'

'Cause?'

'As yet unknown, but we have a clue.' Morrow killed the lights, leaving only the screens and monitors active. His face, reflecting the glow of tell-tales, too on the aspect of a clown's mask; patches of coloured luminescence moving in a drifting pattern of varigated hue. 'Look at the Omphalos, Commander.'

'The Omphalos?'

'The central body – we had to give it a name and this seemed appropriate.'

'The Omphalos – the centre. Koenig looked at it, bright with greenish light, marked, pulsating.

'I'm boosting the registers,' said Morrow. 'Lifting the reception monitors into the ultra-violet and beyond and incorporating a compensatory translator. Now watch!'

The image flickered as he threw switches, the greenish hue changing to a pale violet.

'A beam!' In the shadowed darkness Bergman echoed his amazement. 'We're connected by a beam!'

CHAPTER SEVEN

It rose all around, an inverted cone of shimmering radiance which led from the Moon to a point on the Omphalos. A funnel of sharply defined clarity which joined the two bodies together as a line would join a hooked fish to a rod.

Koenig felt his muscles tighten at the analogy.

'What is this? A freak of some kind? Sandra?'

She too was touched with coloured patches of shifting brightness; reds and blues, greens and yellows from the banked instruments before her touching uniform, hair, face and hands.

'The registers show a directional flow of energy along the beam from us to the Omphalos, Commander. It checks with the observed drain.'

'Victor?' Koenig turned, staring into the darkness, feeling a mounting irritation, one caused by his hampered vision. 'Paul, turn on the lights.' He blinked as Morrow obeyed. 'Well, Victor?'

Bergman said, slowly, 'We can make assumptions, John, but we need more facts. We know that the beam did not originate with us so it is safe to assume that it came from the Omphalos. It could be a natural effect of this space, an automatic discharge-reception such as the exchange of energy between a particle of low potential and one of high. Something similar to a lightning flash, for example.'

'A flash is almost instantaneous.'

'True, but we could be dealing with a temporal vagary – time could appear or actually be different here. In that case an almost instantaneous flash would seem to us to be of long duration.'

'You're guessing, Victor.' Koenig looked at the computer. 'Kano – can you do better?'

'Not me, Commander, but computer – maybe.'

'Try. Find out degrees of probability and waste no time about it. Paul, check every inch of that space out there you can with everything you've got. I want—' Koenig broke off as one of the screens flashed then went blank. 'Trouble?'

'An external scanner burned out.' Morrow made checks and drew in his breath with a sharp inhalation. 'I should have guessed this would happen. The energy drain is affecting our external installations. That particular scanner was close to the defence screen; when it radiated as it did it must have weakened the components and the prevailing drain finished the job.'

'And the others?'

'Already show loss of conversion efficiency, Commander.'

'Have them replaced – all of them. Get on to Maintenance right away. Victor – come with me.'

In his office Koenig sealed the doors cutting him from Main Mission and slumped at his desk. Bergman took a seat facing him and for a moment they looked at each other.

'It's bad, Victor. Right?'

'It could be, John.'

'It is.' Koenig was certain of it, in his heart, head and stomach. The physical signs of an intuition honed by repeated dangers. 'That beam – natural or not it's got us hooked. Maybe that's why we took up an orbit around the Omphalos. That other satellite too, perhaps?' He punched a button and looked at Morrow's face as it appeared on the communications post. 'Paul – a question. Does the planetoid we observed also have a beam connecting it to the Omphalos?'

'It's just come into view, Commander. If you'll hold—' A pause then, 'Yes, it does.'

'Thank you.' Koenig broke the connection and, rising, began to pace the floor. 'An explanation,' he said. 'Victor, give me an explanation.'

'As yet we can only guess, John.'

'Then let us make a start. Here we have a closed system; an area of space which is sealed against the reception of any form of external energy. Any radiated form, that is, we are proof that matter can penetrate. Right?'

Bergman nodded.

'Such an area would, in time, reach entropic death; all energy would have reached a common level and there would be no differing potentials. No life of any kind could exist in such a space, no matter, nothing but a sea of diffused and low-level residue of energy.'

'There is an alternative,' said Bergman. 'A remote possibility that all available energy would become concentrated into a common node. There would still be a run-down, naturally, but instead of a sea of low-order residue there would be a – for want of a better word – a lump of inert mass. Ash, in essence.'

'A magnet,' said Koenig. 'A sponge which would grab every particle of energy that was going. Sucking it into itself like dry ground sucks water. It caught that planetoid and who knows what else beside? Now it's caught us, he added, bitterly. 'Swinging us like an apple on the end of a string. We're trapped in this damned bubble in the sky. Whoever or whatever placed those warnings knew what they were talking about.'

'Death and devastation,' said Bergman, bleakly. 'Death and devastation.'

The loss of all energy, the reduction of matter itself, the end of Alpha and all it contained.

Inevitable – unless somehow they could break free.

The Eagles rose like ungainly wasps; insect-like with the forward vision screen, their armour a natural chitin, their command modules the thorax, the passenger compartments the abdomens.

Their lasers vicious stings.

Carter in command of Eagle One led the other two up and away from the Moon. Below the base rested as if deserted, the buildings masked, the launching pads now empty. Higher and he caught a flash of movement, tiny, suited figures almost invisible against the bleak lunarscape, dimly lit by the greenish luminescence of the Omphalos.

'Service engineers,' said his co-pilot. Frank Dale was young, eager, a little too loquacious, but, at least, he was not a dreamer as Khokol had been. 'A hell of a job – who wants to work on the ground.'

'Someone has to do it.'

'Sure, just as someone has to do the cooking,' agreed Dale. 'I'm just glad that it isn't me.'

Carter said, tersely, 'Check your instrumentation.'

'Sure, Skipper. All systems in the green.'

'Keep them that way.' The pilot pressed a control. 'Report in Eagles Two and Three. Thomson?'

'Everything smooth, Skipper.'

'Kendal?' Carter nodded as a second voice reported that all was well. It should be, all Eagles were kept at the optimum pitch of efficiency, but only a fool would take anything for granted in space. 'Right. Stay in position.' Another switch and Morrow looked from the screen.

'Alan?'

'All set to go. Any alteration in conditions?'

'No. You'd best approach from the side away from the beam. It might be best to leave one Eagle in space in case of—'

'Leave it to me, Paul. I'm the one doing the job.'

And risking his neck. Morrow caught the implication and shrugged. 'So you are, Alan. Did I say you weren't?'

'In as many words – no.'

'So why get annoyed?'

'I'm not.' Carter shook his head. 'I'm edgy, I guess. Sorry, Paul.'

'For what?' Morrow returned Carter's smile. 'It's all yours, Alan. Happy landings.'

'Thanks.'

Carter broke the connection and, as the screen went blank, lifted his eyes to stare through the forward vision ports. Their objective lay ahead, the smooth, slightly glistening ball of the planetoid he was to investigate.

It grew larger as their engines ate the space between them, the dull gleam a little more pronounced but the surface showing no sign of detail. Carter led the flight towards the side away from the Omphalos, staying well clear of the cone he knew connected the two bodies, wary of any stress-fields which might be in the vicinity.

'Thomson?'

'Skipper?'

'You stay in space and maintain observation of immediate area behind and to all sides. Kendal, you hover low but free and keep us in your screens. Report to Main Mission on regular schedule. Understood?'

He smiled at the double agreement, one backed with envy, the other with resignation.

'Don't be jealous, Kendal, you'll get your chance. You too, Thomson. Right, full alert – we're going in.'

Ten minutes later Carter stood on one of the strangest surfaces he had ever known.

It was smooth, that was the most overpowering impression, a ball of rock which had been ground in a gigantic lathe or set to tumble in a drum filled with other objects as large and as hard so that common attrition would wear them into a near-perfect ball. A fantasy which lasted for only a moment then, as Dale came from the grounded Eagle towards him, Carter stooped to kneel, to thrust his helmet close to the ground and to run his gloved hands over the spot before his eyes.

'Skipper?'

'Move three paces to one side and take a sample.' As the co-pilot obeyed Carter spoke again, this time on relay to where Morrow sat in Main Mission. 'Paul? You read me?'

'Yes, go ahead.'

'We've landed and I'm on the surface. It is smooth like a pebble which has been polished. No sign of fusing or of any corrosive forces.'

'Appearance general?'

'Yes. I'm taking samples and will investigate further.'

Carter rose to his feet and stetched, feeling the slight chafe of the suit against his limbs. The enclosing helmet blocked his vision a little so that he had to turn his entire body to see towards the sides, arch his back to stare upwards.

'Dale I'm heading towards the right of the Eagle. Dump the sample and follow.'

He would be ahead but there was no danger of getting lost. Nothing could hide in such a smooth expanse devoid as it was of tree or shrub or even a loose boulder. Like an ant he moved over the sharply curving surface, eyes following the beam of his helmet-light as it threw a cone of brilliance before him.

A light which showed a greyness striated with streaks of dull colour; rust, puce, brown, ochre, madder, indigo, ebon – ebon?

Carter paused and turned and looked again at the black patch which had caught his eye. It rested in a ragged circle a little to one side, the light penetrating it to show walls of a dark olive. A shaft?

'Skipper?' The co-pilot had caught up with him, breathing heavily as though he had been running. 'What's that? A tunnel?'

'Maybe it's only a natural fissure.'

'Maybe.' Dale dropped to his knees at the edge of the opening. 'Hey! It's got grips attached. Metal loops by the look of it. We can climb down.' He added, anxiously, 'We are going to take a look, aren't we?'

They had come to investigate – what else?

Carter led the way, hands gripping the metal hoops which were set too far apart for comfort and too thick for an easy hold. Once his boot slipped and he hung suspended by one hand until he managed to find another hold and to take the strain off his aching shoulders. Below him was nothing but darkness, the beam of his helmet-light seeming to be absorbed by the dull olive of the interior of the shaft. Above, blocked by Dale's body, the ragged circle of the opening grew smaller.

Then a hoop broke and Carter was falling.

'Dale! I—' He landed before he could complete the warning, boots jarring, knees buckling as he dropped to roll, to land hard against a firm surface. A short fall, luckily, frightening in its sheer unexpectedness.

'Skipper? Are you all right?'

'Yes, but watch it. There's a broken hoop. Found it?'

'I – yes. There are others below, still intact.'

'Good. Follow them. It can't be far to the bottom.'

A blur of light and Dale was beside him, breathing a little heavily, leaning back so as to shine his light back up the shaft.

'One broken, Skipper. You were unlucky, but we'll have no trouble climbing back when we want.' The light moved, the bright circle settling in an opening piercing the shaft. 'A passage.'

One ten feet high, the walls rounded, smoothly finished and, like the shaft, of a dull, olive. Carvings marked it, abtruse diagrams which could have been mere accident or deliberate decoration.

Touching them Dale mused, 'I've seen something like this before, Skipper. In a museum one time. They came from Egypt. I forget what they were called.'

'Hieroglyphics.'

'What?'

'Picture writing.'

'Writing?' Dale sucked in his breath. 'What the hell do we have here?'

'I don't know,' said Carter, flatly. 'But we can try to find out.'

The passage curved, fell in a gentle slope, straightened to curve again in a reverse arc to what it had before. Twice Carter halted and attempted to contact the Eagles outside, both times without success.

'Try contacting the relay,' he ordered. 'My radio isn't working.'

'I can hear you.'

'The other frequency. The set may have been damaged when I fell.' He waited then snapped, 'Well?'

'Nothing.' Dale's voice held a shrug. 'Maybe that olive stuff's a barrier of some kind. What is it, anyway? Metal of some kind?'

Carter struck at it with one of the tools clipped to his belt. The edge barely scratched the surface. He tried again, using more force this time, then replaced the tool. Metal or not the stuff was harder than rock and more stubborn than a tempered alloy.

Dale said, 'Skipper, do we go on?'

A decision and Carter knew he had to make it. Safety dictated that he should return, set up a relay-point then recommence the investigation only after making certain that all possible precautions had been made. But Dale, impatient, was already moving down the passage.

For a moment longer Carter hesitated. The matter was urgent, to return and summon the others would take precious time and probably be a waste. This passage would end soon and then would be the time to make decisions.

'Wait!' Carter stepped after the other man. 'Dale, not so fast!'

'Look!' The man had halted to stare at an engraved design. 'Look at that, Skipper! If that isn't a schematic of a rocket-engine I'll eat my helmet! And this – an electronic circuit?'

Accidents, the both of them, a trick of light and an over-active imagination, but there were resemblances and certainly the shaft and passage showed the impact of a sophisticated technology. Someone or something must have built them both and those same people or things could have graced the bare walls with their concept of decoration.

'Let's see what lies lower down.' Dale forged ahead, grunted as the passage forked, unhesitatingly took the left hand corridor.

'Wait!' Carter swore as the other made no answer. 'Dale, blast you, wait!'

The man had gone, racing ahead, following fancied discoveries, moving on before Carter could catch up with him. Turn after turn, the corridors branching, forking, each exactly alike, forming a maze in which Carter realised, too late, they were lost.

'Dale!' He lunged ahead, caught the man's shoulder, pulled him back to slam hard against the wall. 'You fool! Why don't you answer me?'

He saw the startled face beyond the face-plate of the helmet, the moving lips. Metal rang in his ears as he jammed his own helmet against that of his co-pilot.

'Now can you hear me?'

'I – yes. What's the matter, Skipper? The radio—'

'Doesn't work. Or doesn't seem to be working. Check and report. Now!' Carter moved back, lifting his helmet, breaking contact, the bridge over which sound vibration had passed.

Again he saw the lips move but his speakers carried nothing but a soft hum. 'Blast!'

The radios were out, but the silence could be broken. Suits were designed to cater to emergencies and, at times, radio-silence was an advantage when too many men were working in an electronically 'noisy' situation. Carter plucked at his belt, caught the terminal and unreeled the wire from its spool. Plugging it in to Dale's receptor he said, 'Better now?'

'Fine.' The man sighed his pleasure at again being in vocal contact. 'Wonder what killed the radios?'

A question which could wait for an answer. The battery-powered direct connection was, in effect, a telephone and would serve. The next thing to do was to get out of the maze of tunnels.

'This must be an old mine of some kind,' mused Dale. 'Or an underground shelter. 'I've seen pictures of bombproofs and this could be one. Those diagrams could be maps of various sectors and storerooms.' His arm lifted to point. 'That could be one, Skipper. To me it looks like a door.'

The man had sharp eyes. Carter examined the spot, seeing the thin lines tracing an octagonal area, a sunken point containing a knurled wheel surrounded by a ring of individual designs. A combination lock? If so it had to be built by aliens, but all races which used doors and a means to lock them would follow a basic pattern. And unless there were stringent precautions against the practice it might have been as common for them as it was for those of his own kind to make a note of the combination somewhere close.

He found it seven feet from the edge of the door, three symbols which matched those found in the array around the knurled wheel. It moved beneath his gloved hands, turning, a nub halting at each of the symbols in turn. A guess – and Carter glowed to his success.

'You've done it!' Dale stepped forward as the door swung open. 'Skipper, let's look inside!'

They stepped into a mausoleum.

Carter halted, Dale at his side, head and back tilted so as to look up and around. From the high, domed roof hung a mass of delicate, lace-like web, sheets of fine gossamer glowing with refracted colour, hues which faded to burn again only to fade as they shifted the beams of their helmet-lights. Hanging in the webs, folded in it, were tall, fragile shapes with long, pointed skulls and narrow shoulders. The faces were peaked, the eyes enormous beneath protruding brows, the hands long-fingered with nails of pearl. Each hand held seven fingers and each finger was jointed in four places.

'Dead!' whispered Dale. 'They're all dead.'

They had been dead for eons. Even as they watched a body fell from where it hung suspended in the web which had served as a shroud, bones shattering to add their substance to the pile below, a heap of greyish dust which rose beneath the impact to settle in a slightly wider pattern.

The floor was covered with the dust, the accumulated debris of ages.

'Webs.' Dale moved, guiding his light, the circle of brilliance probing the rear of the cavern. 'Spiders, maybe?'

'No.'

'Why not?'

'Look at the bodies. None touched or eaten. Those webs weren't spun by spiders.'

Not unless the bodies now suspended had stemmed from an arachnid ancestry, the extra limbs absorbed as mankind had absorbed the gills it had once known, shed the tail it no longer needed. And who could tell of the customs and ways of an alien race? They had lived and built and tried to survive with tunnels and sealed chambers and, perhaps, mystic signs scratched on the adamantine walls of their defences. They had failed and had withdrawn to spend the last moments of their lives in communion with each other, gathering to fashion their webs, to hang in them, to die in them.

Their equivalent of beds, perhaps, of couches.

Of tombs.

Carter moved a little, looking at a pathetic tableau; two adult shapes together with two smaller ones of unequal size. A family group gathered together for mutual comfort? The hands were interlocked, the huge eyes open, pale and desiccated orbs which one, perhaps, had known the bitterness of tears.

'Skipper?' Dale was uneasy. 'This place is giving me the creeps. How about getting the hell out of here?'

Another body fell as he spoke, landing close by to dissolve into dust, adding more bulk to the powder which littered the floor. Another, two at a time, a sudden fall of withered figures like a ghastly rain.

'The floor! It's moving!' Carter turned towards the entrance. 'The door! It's closed!'

More than the floor had moved. The slight tremor had swung the door on its gimbals, sending it to fit snugly into the opening.

Even before he reached it Carter knew that, somehow, it had locked itself.

That he and Dale were sealed in with the alien dead.

CHAPTER EIGHT

Tony Ellman staggered and almost fell, regaining his balance with a tremendous effort, uneasily aware of the jagged rocks at his feet, the danger of smashing his face-plate, of dying in the airless void.

'Tony?' Nyat Cheng's voice, concerned as it came from the radio. 'You all right?'

'Fine.'

'You sure?'

'Sure I'm sure!' Anger edged his reply. Why the hell couldn't Cheng mind his own business? The day he needed mothering would be the day. 'I'm fine,' he said again. 'Now let's quit worrying about me and get on with the job. Right?'

'Maybe you should report back in?'

'No!'

'I think you should.' The overseer's voice held determination. 'Get back to the bug, Tony, and take it easy. That's an order.'

'You know what you can do with it?'

'Now you listen—'

'No! You listen! This is an emergency job, right? It needs to be done and fast – that's what emergency means. Now you stick to your job and let me get on with mine.' He added, grimly, 'I mean it, Nyat. Come near me and I'll brain you and that goes for anyone else who thinks I'm getting past it.'

A challenge and a stupid one, why had he given it? Would he really fight if anyone came close. Only an idiot would attempt to struggle outside on the Lunar plain when too many little things could cause a ruptured suit and burst lungs. But why the hell couldn't they leave him alone?

He sighed, rising to straighten his back, conscious of the ache, the drag of weary muscles. Damn the hospital and the doctors – he hadn't felt right since they'd done that series of tests on him after Sam had died. And that was another thing. Sam shouldn't have died. They should have looked after him. Sam had been one of the best. He missed him.

Irritably Ellman shook his head. What was the matter with him? Sam was dead – so what? Everyone had to die and some had the luck to go early and others had to wait. What you lost one way you made up in another. Die young and you dodged the aches and pains of growing old, the failing of natural attributes, the growing inadequacy. Die old and you gained the extra joys of youth.

Why was he thinking about dying when work waited to be done?

Turning he looked around. Nyat Cheng was way over towards the base; apparently he'd given up and was saving further argument until they had finished their stint. A couple of others were in view both hard at work. Ellman aimed his drill, leaned on it, tripped the mechanism. Chips of rock flew from beneath the point, deepening the hole from which he'd removed the scanner. It was oddly erroded, the lens scarred, the metal surround looking as if it had been abraded with something like an emery-blast. The replacement would be set deeper with a new, wide angle lens fitted with a removable cover of transparent plastic.

Setting aside the drill Ellman crouched, fighting a sudden giddiness. He was an electronics man and a good one. Testing his work was a waste of time; each connection was firm, every terminal correct, and when he did a layout everything was as it should be. To him it was a matter of pride that it was.

A small thing, perhaps, but important to both himself and to Alpha.

Now he swore as his gloved hands were slow to obey his mental commands. The wires fell, were recovered, failed to click home. He paused, squeezing shut his eyes before trying again. He was tired, a treble shift was enough to take it out of a giant, but working was better than waiting and if he could do nothing else he could work.

'Get in!' he muttered. 'Damn you, get in!' Again the wires slipped. There was too little slack, the junctions were awkwardly placed, the connections too tight, the design a lousy combination of some nut-dreamer and a moronic engineer. Why the hell couldn't they build stuff a man could use? 'Get in! In!'

He siged with relief as the terminals clicked home. A tug to test, a check for fit and the scanner was back in its hole, aligned on its guides, ready to operate as it should.

Chalk up one more success.

His head reeled as he climbed to his feet, the Lunar plain turning, twisting, heaving as if with a life of its own.

'Tony!' Cheng had been watching. He began to run as the distant figure swayed. 'Move in, Gerry. Fast!'

'Got it, Nyat.' Gerry Ross lunged forward as fast as safety would allow. He was close when Ellman began to fall, closer when he spun, to topple, to land with a horrible gasping.

The more horrible sound of escaping air.

'His face-plate!' He reached the fallen man, one hand tearing at the emergency patches attached to his thigh, ripping free the adhesive-backed plastic and holding ready as he turned the limp figure. His guess had been wrong, the helmet was intact, the rupture at a point close to the junction with the suit. A jagged shard of rock had ripped through the tough material.

'Quick!' Cheng had poined him. 'The patch, man! The patch!'

The air-hiss died as it was slapped home but the horror remained.

'His face!' Ross swallowed as he looked at it. 'His face, Cheng! Look at his face!'

Age can bring beauty but only when it is the natural achievement of the passage of time. A wall, mellowed, graced with lichens, hard lines and edges worn and smoothed beneath the hand of years. A garden, grown in harmony, each plant settled in an area hard-won and now its own, colours blending, leaves interwound, a whole where there had once been only parts; those parts now blended and matured with the passing of numerous seasons. Such things held beauty but age, gained without reason, was something else.

Helena Russell stared at horror.

A horror implied, not actual, for there was nothing really horrible about a face which had grown the deep lines and creped skin of advancing years. Nothing dreadful at seeing the natural state of all living things providing they manage to survive long enough. No doctor could ever find the relentless workings of katabolism strange and fearful. Men were born, they lived, they grew old, they died. It was the way of the human race.

The horror lay in the unusual.

Tony Ellman was thirty-two years of age.

Now he looked eighty.

He *was* eighty.

Mathias was in no doubt.

'Every test proves it, Doctor; blood, marrow, hormones, lymphatic fluids – the man is senile.'

'How?' Then, as he made no answer, she asked again, more savagely this time, 'How did it happen? How?'

'I don't know.'

'But—'

'You asked how it happened and I gave you a truthful reply. I don't know *how* it happened, but I do know it is an extension of previous discoveries. Accelerated aging, Doctor, a speeded breakdown in the metabolism which leads to inevitable senility.' He added, quietly, 'You saw the results of my tests. You made checks yourself. What we suspected then is now a fact.'

One she was reluctant to accept and still questions remained – ones which could be answered.

'Ellman was a patient together with Sam Blake. He was under observation for strained ligaments and a cartilage operation on the knee. Healing was slow, but not extremely slow.'

'As it was with Blake,' Mathias admitted. 'A connection?'

'Both were outside workers. Both could have been exposed to an area of intensive radiation of some kind. I'm guessing,' she confessed. 'No radiation should cause such results; superficial injury, cellular breakdown, cancer, eventual death, yes, but senility?'

'Senility is the breakdown of all normal physical functions coupled with mental aberration,' Mathias reminded. 'A deranged mind could contribute to the result by failure to maintain control over the bodily processes. Exposure to radiation could easily cause cortical degeneration.'

'And eventual physical breakdown,' said Helena. 'But the time element, Bob? This man aged in a matter of hours. He was apparently fit when he commenced his tour of duty and yet, when found, he was in the last stages of exhaustion. He was suited, isolated and yet, somehow, he aged fifty years.'

And was still aging. Helena glanced at the monitors then through the transparent partition to where Tony Ellman lay in the intensive care unit. The lighting was dim, rich in ultra violet, the bluish glow giving his skin the waxen appearance of a corpse. His cheeks were sunken, closed eyes resting in bruised sockets, folds of skin hanging from his jowls. His hands, thin and fragile, rested on his lap. The bulk of the life-support apparatus covering his torso hid any motion of his chest and only the winking tell-tales showed that he was still alive.

'He's going to die, Bob,' she said, bleakly. 'There's nothing we can do to save him.'

A patient lost and one who would not be allowed to rest in peace. Dead he could still talk; with his tissues, glands, bones and brain. With scraps of internal organs, ligaments, sinews, membranes, skin. Items which would be taken and tested and wrung for information. The last service to Alpha Tony Ellman would ever make.

Mathias said, thoughtfully. 'He was prone – it has to be the explanation. Triggered and primed by his earlier exposure. Then, when he went outside he was ready to go. The treble shift did it and, once started, the aging process was geometrical.'

Two becoming four becoming eight becoming sixteen becoming thirty-two – how long would it take for enough cells to die of senility to become obvious? All too soon, she thought. Once started the process would rage through normal tissue like fire through a corn field ready for harvest.

Helena lifted the commlock from her belt.

'Get me the Commander.' A moment then, as Koenig's face appeared on the screen, she said, 'This is urgent, John. I have to see you.'

'Can't it wait?'

'No.' His face and tone betrayed the tension he was under. 'No,' she said again. 'It can't wait.'

'Join me in my office in ten minutes.' Then, before breaking the connection, he added, 'What is it about?'

'Us, John. All of us in Alpha – we are all facing premature death!'

'Age!' Victor Bergman lifted his hands and looked at them. Broad, capable, the backs marked with brown splotches, the knuckles prominent, the nails neatly filed and polished. 'There's no doubt, Helena?'

'None.' Her eyes moved from Bergman's hands to Koenig's eyes. 'Ellman died just after I called you and Bob's doing the autopsy at this moment, but we know what he will find. Death caused by senility – I won't bother you with the medical jargon. Just say that he died of old age.'

'He was a young man.'

'Was, John.' She emphasised the past tense. 'But not now. Something outside drained the life from his body as if he were water and it a sponge.' She caught his change of expression. 'John?'

'Nothing.' He saw her determination and shrugged. 'It was just the analogy you used – water and a sponge. I've used it myself.'

'Age,' said Bergman again. He lowered his hands. 'A sudden acceleration in the metabolic breakdown, Helena. Am I correct?'

'Yes.'

'Caused by some external force?'

She nodded, sensing there was more to the question, something which, as yet, she didn't understand.

Bergman said, quietly, 'It fits the pattern, John. Life is a form of energy and one more subject to destruction than most. Ellman was somehow more sensitive than the rest. His insistence of working the treble shift was symptomatic of his condition – a sudden and final blaze of energy similar to the glow of a fire fanned by a wind, brightening before the last of its fuel is exhausted. How long do we have, Helena?'

He was the oldest and would have the greater personal concern and Helena remembered the way he had lifted his hands as if to study them. A natural reaction – what man could tamely ignore the approach of extinction? It was hard not to be able to give comfort.

'I don't know as yet, Victor, but it can't be long. We were still running tests when Ellman collapsed and had determined that there was a general attrition of the metabolism giving a preponderance to the katabolic factors. Ellman aged fifty years in a matter of hours so, obviously, there must be a collapse-point. It is probably a variable governed by the individual resistance of each individual – but all will be affected.'

Koenig said, 'Is there anything we can do? Some protection we can adopt?'

'All I can suggest is that none of those working with Ellman be permitted to leave the shelter of the base. They should be found work in the lower levels. In fact it would be best if everyone were to be kept deep beneath the rock. It might help.'

'I doubt it.' Koenig told her of the mysterious beam and energy loss. 'The same analogy, Helena – water and a sponge. We're the water and the Omphalos is the sponge. Now it seems it wants to suck up more than we can afford to give. Could there be a connection?'

'Perhaps, but I'll have to make tests to be sure. Cultures could be set and exposed and checks made to see how the bacteria progress. But, John, can't we use the defence shield? Won't it protect us?'

Using it would cost energy, but at least it might buy them time. Koenig rose and led the way into Main Mission.

'Upper register, Paul. Let's see that beam.'

He heard Helena inhale as it appeared on the screens, lambent, cold, hungry.

'Up shield!'

As it rose, shimmering, scintillating with a brilliant coruscation of sparkling energy, Sandra Benes reported from her station.

'Energy loss thirty-nine per cent, Commander.'

'Boost to three-quarters full! Sandra?'

'Fifty-seven per cent total loss.'

More than half their generated power streaming wastefully

into space. Koenig snapped, 'Full power, Paul. Hold until I give word to lower.'

He blinked as the shield blazed with sudden and savage fury, light and brilliance turning the connecting beam into a glowing cone, solidifying it as dust would a beam of light.

'Commander!'

The internal lights dimmed as Morrow gave the warning. An alarm sounded, another, warnings that the base was dying, the power which was its life drained from the machines essential to survival.

'Commander! You must—'

'Cut!' Koenig anticipated the demand. 'Sandra?'

'Power restored. Loss now registering at twenty-two per cent.'

Higher than before and it would mount. Time was against them in more ways than one. Trapped, dying, their energy draining away – how long could they last?

CHAPTER NINE

In the darkness something moved; a bulky shape which reflected glitters, the helmet staring with its single eye, dust rising from beneath the boots. Alan Carter watched it, noting how the beam of Dale's light caught the hanging webs and turned them into fairy-shimmers of gossamer rainbows. Sparkling curtains blotched with the suspended dead which hung like dried fruit on the fronds of some ailen plant.

Like flies caught and drained and left as desiccated husks by some monstrous spider.

An unpleasant analogy and one too close to the truth. There was no spider and this chamber was no lair. The dead had not been drained by slavering fangs. The darkness held no alien peril.

But death, when it came, would be just as real.

Irritably Carter shook his head and, rising from where he squatted, waited for Dale to join him. For a moment he fumbled then the connection snapped into place and they could talk again.

'Anything?'

'No.' Dale was curt. 'I moved all around the edge of the floor – it was solid all the way. Lots of dust and some boxes. A litter of fragments which could have been anything. I didn't waste time examining them.'

'No traps?'

'I told you – nothing.' Over the phone Carter could hear the man take a deep breath and, when he next spoke, his voice held a forced lightness. 'Well, Skipper, I guess this is it, right?'

'Wrong.'

'You're an optimist. The doors sealed, the chamber is solid, the radios don't work so we can't call for help – are you hoping for a miracle?'

'We're not dead yet,' said Carter. 'And while there's life—'

'— there's hope.' Dale finished the quotation. 'They used to teach me that at Sunday School but I never managed to figure out just what it meant. Hope for what? Me, I'd settle for a radio that worked or a mining drill which could drill a way out of here, or a rescue party suddenly appearing right in front of us. Hope!' His voice held a shrug. 'Maybe we should just sit down and pray?'

Carter said, flatly, 'I've done that. Now let's take another look at that door.'

It was as they had left it, a metal slab firmly set in the octagonal jamb. The inner wheel bore the same ring of symbols but, no matter how he turned it, Carter hadn't been able to swing it free. Now he tried again, trying to remember the exact sequence he had used before. A double wriggle like a twisted helix, an interwound line, a pattern of superimposed stars.

The door stayed sealed.

'Something must have closed it,' said Dale. 'But what?'

'We know what closed it.' Carter turned the knurled wheel, trying again. With three symbols there would have been six possible combinations. The marked ring held fifteen – it could take a thousand years to hit the correct sequence by trial and error. 'We felt the shift of the floor. The planetoid must have tilted a little on its axis.'

Only a little but it would have been enough to swing shut the counterbalanced door. To turn the chamber of the dead aliens into a human tomb.

'Let me try,' said Dale as Carter dropped his hands from the wheel. 'Maybe I can hit it.'

'Keep trying,' said Carter. 'I'm going to take a look around.'

He jerked free the connecting wire and let it wind back on its spring-loaded spool. Now the silence within his helmet was broken only by the sound of his own breathing, the gentle susurration of circulating air. Normally the sound was almost inaudible, noticed only when absent, now it had grown to dominate all others.

When it ceased he would die.

A matter neither of them had mentioned because each knew it too well. Death waited, not in the alien chamber, but in their own air tanks. It grew as the oxygen diminished, would strike when the last dregs had been used, would claim its own when asphyxiated, they succumbed to the final, eternal darkness.

He stumbled and almost fell, regaining his balance to look down to where a tangle of metal rods lay at his feet. Stooping he picked them up, turning them, studying their arrangement. Loops and eyes and interlocking bars forming a peculiar combination of unknown purpose. A toy? An instrument of some kind? A religious object? Discarded junk? How to read an alien mind?

Carter moved on, turning once to look at Dale where he stood before the door, reflected light haloing helmet and suit and turning him into a bizarre presentation of the human shape.

The juncture of the walls and floor was, he knew, solid. Previous investigations had shown the floor to be the same. Higher, beyond reach, darkness ran from the moving circle of his light, the webs casting lacey shadows, colours sparkling to fade and die, to return with swathes of sombre hue.

Webs which had to be suspended from something. The rods he had found, perhaps?

Carter knelt, rolled on to his back, stared upwards towards the roof as he inched himself across the dust. A race which used webs as couches could have had an avian ancestry – certainly they would have had little fear of heights. Living in a practically three-dimensional area doors and entrances would be placed without regard to the factors which guided human use. Perhaps, beyond the range of his vision, another opening could be found.

Dale turned as Carter slapped his hand on the other's helmet. Once connected he said, 'No luck, Skipper. The wheel just turns and turns. I've tried until I'm dizzy.'

'Sit down. Rest a while. Step up the oxygen.'

They had cut down the flow to conserve supplies but had paid for it with rapid fatigue and a slowness of mental aptitude. Now, as they squatted, Carter opened his valve and watched as Dale did the same.

'How long, Skipper?'

He was talking about their life expectancy but Carter deliberately misunderstood.

'Not long. Kendal knows we went down the shaft. He knows

we've broken communication. He'll come looking for us.'

'And find what?' Dale snorted. 'There's a maze outside that door so how can he trail us? And even if he could how can he know we're behind that door? And even if he does know how can he open it?'

'The trouble with you,' said Carter, 'is that you're a pessimist. Look on the bright side. We are alive, we have air, we have our brains and we have help coming from outside. It's just a matter of time.'

'So why am I worried?'

'I told you; it's because you're a pessimist. An optimist now, well, he would say that we've a nice, snug place to sit in, interesting things to see, a little problem to solve and so exercise our brains, and a story to tell our grandchildren.'

'Skipper, you're a fool,' said Dale, but his tone was lighter than it had been. The graveyard humour had worked for this time at least, but Carter knew that it wouldn't continue to dispel the inevitable fear and depression the future would bring. The panic too, perhaps, the one thing above all they had to guard against.

He said, 'Dale, I've been thinking. These people must have come in here for safety. The door was sealed – so why isn't there any air?'

For a moment the co-pilot remained silent then he grunted. 'No air? Of course! Why didn't I think of that?'

'Think of it now,' urged Carter. It would be better if Dale could provide the answers. 'No air – why?'

'It could have leaked. This place is old and over the years it could have seeped away.'

'Possible,' admitted Carter, 'but this chamber is lined with the same olive metal as the shaft and tunnels. As far as we can see it's intact. And look at the dust, if there had been a trace of air when we opened the door it would have blown towards us. It didn't.'

'So this place was a vacuum when we found it.' Dale was thoughtful. 'A fissure, maybe? A crack leading outside?'

'That or another door – an open door.'

'A way out!' Dale sucked in his breath. 'Skipper, you're a

genius. Now tell me where it's to be found.'

'Up,' said Carter. 'Somewhere up high. It has to be.'

In the mirror the face was smooth, the skin clear, marked only by the thin lines of character, the mould of muscle and bone. How long would it be before age marred the contours, sagged the flesh, turned the present features into a raddled mask?

Thinking of it Helena Russell lifted a hand and touched the mane of golden hair, soon to turn white, to grow brittle, to hang in stringy tufts from the dome of her scalp. To grow old was nothing given the time to do it. But if she, suddenly, became a thing of senility and decay . . .

The hum of her commlock broke the train of thought and she lifted the instrument from her belt, glad of the interruption, the electronic contact with others of her kind.

Koenig looked at her from the screen. He was worried.

'Helena, some trouble. Alan and his co-pilot are missing. At least they are out of contact.'

'Missing?' She remembered the mission he had led. 'On the planetoid?'

'He found a shaft of some kind and investigated it. Radio contact was lost. Kendal waited and then landed to search. He found a maze of tunnels.'

'And Alan?'

'No sign of either he or Dale. They might be in need of emergency medical assistance. If you would ask Bob—'

'No,' she interrupted. 'There's no need for that. I'll meet you on the launching pad in five minutes.'

'Helena—'

'Don't waste time arguing, John. Five minutes.'

Bergman was seated in the passenger module when she arrived. He saw her expression and guessed what was in her mind.

'No one can live forever, Helena.'

'But this is stupid, Victor. You aren't needed. You should be staying in the lowest depths of Alpha.'

'Where I'd be safe?' He smiled as she made no answer. 'And what about you?'

'I'm a doctor. It's my job.'

'It could be mine. Kendal reported a strange olive-coloured metallic-seeming coating lining the shaft and tunnels. It appears to have been placed by an intelligent race. I want to see it, to examine it and learn what I can. As we can't bring the planetoid to me then I must go to the planetoid.' He grunted as the Eagle lifted, Koenig at the controls. 'And don't worry about my health. I think that the aging process is a direct result of the beam impinging on the Moon from the Omphalos. We'll be away from it within seconds.'

A comfort – why had she been so terrified of sudden age? An instinctive rejection of the lost opportunities? Anger at the years lost and never lived? A woman's vanity?

She thought of Koenig and tried to imagine his face seamed and lined and creped as Ellman's had been. His shoulders stooped, his limbs wasted, his bones grown brittle, his sharp intellect reduced to senseless wanderings.

It would come. Given time it would come – why did life have to be so short?

Bergman shrugged as she put the question, 'Helena, for some men eternity isn't long enough and for others a decade is too long. Who can tell? Personally I hope to live long enough to see we Alphans settled on a new world. Once that has been accomplished, well, we all have to go and, for me, that will be as good a time as any.'

To find a new Earth – the hope and dream of them all. To find a world on which they could settle and build and be safe from the perils which menaced them in space. But perhaps they had already left it too late. The doom they had escaped in the past now waited for them here in this alien space. A death from which there seemed to be no escape.

Depressed she leaned back as the Eagle hurtled through space. From the pilot's seat Koenig said, 'Better check your equipment, Helena. Minutes could count.'

His voice was flat, emotionless, but she could guess his concern.

'It's been done, John. When do we land?'

'Soon.' The throb of the engines at full power underlined his terseness. 'Kendal will be waiting.'

He stood, suited, his co-pilot beside him on the smooth expanse of the planetoid. Carter's Eagle was to his rear, the open hole of the shaft at his feet. He gestured towards it as Koenig and the others came towards him.

'This is it, Commander. I've scanned the area and found no other opening. If they came out at all it had to be from here.'

'And they didn't?'

'No.' Kendal was positive. 'I've been operating continuous scan.'

'And?'

'I warned Thomson and went after them. As I reported there's a maze down there. The tunnels are lined with metal of some kind which seems to act as a radio-barrier.' The man realised he was repeating himself, wasting time relaying information which they already knew. 'Your orders?'

'We go down. Signal Thomson to hover low and maintain general watch.' Koenig forced himself to contain his impatience. 'Then follow us down. But waste no time.'

Hurry before the store of air was exhausted and the need for rescue had passed. Before the men died from lack of oxygen and the base had lost two good workers, before he lost an old and valued friend.

Bergman grunted as he landed at the foot of the shaft. Metal glinted in his hand as he scratched at the olive surface.

'This colouring is like a patina, John. Similar to that found on bronze. Beneath the metal is incredibly hard and dense. It would be interesting to discover how it was worked.'

'Later.' Koenig was following Kendal's co-pilot along the passage. 'Helena, stay close.'

She came after him, her medical bag slung over her shoulder, Koenig carrying the more bulky equipment; the sac which could be sealed around the doctor and her patient, inflated so as to permit her to remove a suit and give emergency treatment if necessary.

'We left a trail,' explained Shaw, the co-pilot. 'See?' He pointed to a thin line of white powder which lay on the floor. 'And we left other marks on the walls ahead. If you want to keep in touch you'd better make wire-connections now.'

A few moments and it was done, Koenig thinning his lips at the essential delay.

'Did you find anything other than passages? Traps, alcoves, chambers?'

'No, Commander.'

'Any upward-leading shafts?'

'No.' Shaw grunted as he bumped into a wall. 'Nothing.'

An answer which made no sense. Men couldn't simply vanish without cause. The corridors seemed solid, the floor, the roof. The tunnels, branching and forking, formed an intricate maze but with the white powder tracing their path and marks on the walls they were covering every foot.

Koenig halted as he saw whiteness in the beam of his light. 'We've covered this part.'

'There's another passage to the right,' said Bergman. He headed towards it, the connecting wire growing taut slackening as he halted. 'We've covered that too. John, there has to be something we haven't spotted as yet. A room in which they are trapped, maybe. A chute down which they have fallen. They could be inches from us. On the other side of a wall.'

But without a means of communication they would never know.

And both air and time were running out.

Dale sagged, the sound of his breathing harsh, ragged, a wheeze in his throat and lungs. 'No,' he said. 'Damn it, Skipper, no. There isn't a door. There isn't even a hole large enough to pass a cat. You were wrong.'

Wrong, thought Carter bleakly, but not wholly so. He looked at the thin crack in the circle of light thrown by his helmet, the only flaw in the walls and roof they had found. A small thing, barely noticeable, one they would not have discovered at all if it hadn't been for the five bodies lying beneath it, the clutter of interwound rods.

A ladder the dead had tried to use in a final attempt to seal the crack.

One which had bled the air from the chamber in a slow but relentless harbinger of death.

His boot hit a heap of dust as he turned and led the way back towards the door. Grit flew and something hard rolled to settle a few feet ahead. Stooping he picked it up and rolled it in his gloved hand. A stone, elaborately carved, set in a curved band of metal. A bracelet or an arm band. An item of jewellery once prized and now less than rubbish.

Carter slipped it over his forearm, the metal hitting the power-pack on his belt as he lowered his hand, a sharp click sounding in his helmet.

Dale said, 'What was that, Skipper?'

'What?'

'A click. I heard it through my phones.'

'You did?' Carter frowned, trying to think and finding it difficult. The air, he knew, it was too vitiated; too rich in waste and too low in oxygen. The result of deliberately adjusting the valves. Extra life had been gained at the expense of mental alertness.

'A click.' Dale was insistent. To him in his low condition it had become a very important problem to be painstakingly solved. 'In my phones. In my phones, Skipper.'

Carter looked down at his belt. The power-pack fitted snugly, the batteries at almost full charge. He hit it again with the metal band and then, with sudden clarity, was jerking at the catches.

'Skipper?' Dale caught at his arm. 'You crazy or something?'

'No.'

'Then—'

'They're out there looking for us, right? The Commander,' he yelled as Dale made no answer. 'Kendal and the others. They can't be far but they can't hear us. We've no radio.'

'So?'

'We'll make noise. They must be using phones if they're in the tunnels. Now listen.' He touched the band to the battery terminals, creating an arc, a minute flare which caused a crackle in his earphones. 'Old-fashioned radio,' he said. 'A spark gap. They can't pick it up on UHF but it might trigger their phones. All we need is to create noise.' He manipulated the band, concentrating on his fingers, the sound which buzzed from his phones. Three shorts, three longs, three shorts. SOS. The old call for help in a code developed long before he'd been born. 'Get it, Dale?'

'I get it.' The man slumped against the door. His voice was tired, slurred. 'Morse Code. Can I help, Skipper? Can I—'

'You can sit, save your breath and hang on. And,' Carter added, grimly, 'you can pray someone hears us.'

A prayer that was answered.

Koenig frowned as his phones buzzed, the sound repeated to form a pattern.

'John!' Helena turned to face him. 'What—?'

'Silence!' He held up one hand. 'All of you, be quiet and listen.' He held his breath as the buzzing continued. 'It's code.'

'A call for help, John.' Bergman threw his light against the walls around them. 'From the missing men, obviously, but where are they?'

'A door,' snapped Koenig. 'Look for a door.'

Helena found it, spotting the thin lines depicting the octagonal opening, catching the outline in a shift of the light. Koenig dropped to his knees and lowered his helmet to the floor. Staring over the surface he saw little scuffs in the fine tracery of dust.

'This is it. Victor, how can we get it open?'

Bergman said, dubiously, 'I'm not sure, John. We'll need lasers and drills at least. If we try to blow it open we could kill the others. If we could only talk to them perhaps they could tell us how they got inside.'

Shaw had brought a heavy crowbar with him. Koenig took it, lifted it, sent it smashing hard against the door. Three times he repeated the blows then paused. The impact would be unheard unless one or the other was in direct contact with the metal, but the chance was worth taking. After a moment he repeated the blows, paused, slammed at the metal again.

Inside the chamber Dale stirred and said, 'Skipper, my head. I keep getting sounds in my head.'

'Clicks?'

'No.' Clumsily Dale moved, his suited figure rolling away from the door against which he had been leaning. 'Thuds like a hammer was at work. A hammer,' he muttered and then, suddenly, retched. 'Air – I've gotta have air!'

He was dying. Had he been deep in water he would have inhaled his lungs full of liquid, impelled by the sheer necessity to breathe, a reflex over which he would no longer have control. As it was, in the suit, he could do nothing but gasp and flounder like a landed fish, inhaling stale poison, trying to rid himself of it, in danger of strangling on his own vomit.

Kneeling Carter spun the valves, flushing out the air cylinder and feeding the last puff of precious oxygen to the helpless man.

It was impossible to do more. His own supply was exhausted, only a difference in metabolism had enabled him to last a little longer. Tiredly he leaned back against the door, the crude signals forgotten as he rested his helmet against the metal.

And heard the repeated thud of blows.

'Dale! They're here! They're outside! Hold on, man! Hold on!'

The band slipped in his fingers, almost fell, lifted as if it weighed a ton to touch the terminals and to flash its spark and electronic noise. Not to call for help, that had arrived, but to relay the most important information of all.

'Door . . . wheel . . . combolock,' he muttered as his fingers spelt out the words. 'Wriggle . . . coil . . . stars. Sequence . . . helix . . . twist . . . stars. Door . . . wheel . . . lock – for God's sake hurry!'

The thud of blows signalling what? Agreement, understanding, mystification? Had they heard at all? Could they hear? Would the door open if they could?

The band fell and he picked it up, darkness edging his vision, the sour taste of acid in his throat, pain growing in his lungs. He retched, spattering the interior of his helmet with a thin wetness then retched again, dry heaves which tore at his lungs and sent stars to flame in ruby dartings against the growing darkness.

Dying.

He was dying!

And then, suddenly, there was peace.

CHAPTER TEN

Helena said, sharply, 'The tanks, quickly!'

Bergman was already at work kneeling beside one of the sprawled figures, his hands deft as he undid the connection and fitted the new container of air. A twist of the valve and oxygen gusted into the suit, chilling but carrying with it the essence of life. To one side Helena was doing the same, checking, probing, her fingers searching for signs of life as her eyes checked monitors.

'Victor?'

'Nothing.' He stared through the soiled face-plate and saw the starting eyes, the tongue, the distorted features. 'This is Dale. He's dead.'

'And Alan?' Koenig stood by the open door, cursing the delay it had caused. A few minutes earlier and both would have been safe. A little faster in solving the crude message – but to regret was useless, time could not be reversed, what had happened was done. 'Helena?'

'The sac,' she snapped. 'Quickly!'

In such matters she was to be obeyed. Koenig ripped open the emergency pack, wrapped the thin but tough membrane around both Helena and the still figure at her side, threw in her medical bag and a spare tank of air. Sealing the bag he twisted the valve of the cylinder, pressure rounding the sac as it filled with air.

Inside Helena set to work.

The suit had been flushed but Alan hadn't responded. He was, she decided, medically dead. His lungs had ceased to work and his heart to beat – unless the flow of blood could be restored to his brain within minutes he would, if he lived at all, be a mental cripple, the lack of oxygen having caused irremediable damage.

Minutes – and he had been dead for how long?

The helmet came free and was thrown to one side. Quickly

she wiped the mouth and chin and held the nozzle of the air tank to flaccid lips. Propping it into position she moved to straddle the supine figure and, stiffening her arms, threw her weight against the torso in the region of the heart. The suit hampered her and made it difficult to hit the right spot, but practice had earned her skill and the heels of her hands slammed up beneath the ribs as she massaged the heart.

As he made no response she paused and took a hypodermic from her bag. It was loaded with a heavy dose of adrenalin and ready to fire its charge into the bloodstream. She triggered it, sending the drug into the great veins of the neck and again thrust her hands against the torso.

A minute gone at least, maybe two.

'Alan! Alan Carter! Alan!'

He lay as if dead. He was dead and only she could restore him. She had unsealed her helmet, lifting the faceplate, and now she stooped over the still figure. Inflating her chest she adjusted his head then, parting his lips, pressed her own against them and gusted air into the pilot's lungs.

Again.

Again.

Inhale, blow, release, inhale, blow, release . . . pumping air into him as if he were a balloon.

The kiss of life and the only chance he had.

Again she massaged the heart, again breathed into him, her mouth against his own.

'Alan! For God's sake! Alan!'

Carter stirred, moaned a little, sucked air into his lungs. Helena straightened, still straddled across his body, her helmet touching the top of the sac. From her bag she took a phial and sprayed an acrid compound into his mouth and nostrils. He coughed, choked a little and opened his eyes.

'Alan. Do you know who you are?'

'I—' His eyes rolled a little, vague, empty. 'Who? What? You—'

She said again, her voice holding the sting of a whip, 'Who are you? Tell me who you are!'

The essential test of identity. He could have been dead too

long, the ego already impaired, his personality changed, blurred, distorted. If so it were better that she had let him go. Kinder to give him an injection now and report that she had been too late.

Not that she would need to lie. Koenig, for one, would understand.

'Alan?'

'Doctor!' His eyes settled, became bright with life and awareness. 'Doctor Russell!'

'Who are you? Tell me?' She relaxed as he obeyed, adding other information, proving that his intelligence was unimpaired. 'Relax,' she ordered as he moved beneath her thighs. 'Don't try to move just yet. Just lie and breathe and let your heart and lungs achieve full automatic operation.'

'I'm all right, Doctor.'

'Yes, thank God!'

Her tone betrayed her and, staring up into her face Carter said, slowly, 'It was close, eh? I'd passed out. I remember that I was retching then seemed to be falling and then there was nothing. It was odd in a way. As if, at the end, nothing really mattered. That all the struggle and fear was over. And then—' He broke off then added, slowly, 'I was dead. Dead and you resurrected me.'

Her hand reached for another hypodermic, this one loaded with a tranquiliser. She had won the battle with death before and knew what could so easily happen. The resurgence of life, the euphoria, the biological reaction which affected men and women alike and was the most common cause of romantic associations formed by patients for their doctors and nurses.

Carter saw the instrument in her lifted hand and said, dryly, 'You know, Doctor, this is getting to be a habit. If it keeps up I'll be so compromised that you'll have to marry me.'

A joke and his way of telling her that the danger she feared did not exist, that he needed no chemical help to regain his normal emotional equilibrium.

Then, as she restored the hypodermic to her bag, he said, 'I was lucky. You got to me in time. But Dale? What about Dale?'

He was dead, inert flesh locked in a personal coffin, the suit which had maintained his life now a temporary grave. Koenig watched him leave, carried in Kendal's Eagle together with Helena and her patient. Carter had sworn that he was fit for duty but Koenig had insisted and he'd had no choice but to obey.

As the Eagle dwindled and vanished from sight he turned to where Bergman was kneeling, his gloved hands probing at the ground.

'Have you noticed anything strange about this place, John?'

'It's small and round and apparently smooth,' said Koenig and added, dryly, 'I've been a little too busy to pay much attention to the scenery.'

'The chamber.' Bergman rose. 'And that metal lining the tunnels. The inscriptions too, all most interesting.'

And food for later study if ever they had the time or opportunity. Already Thomson's co-pilot had taken a series of photographs and was even now attempting to remove a segment of the stuff from the rim of the shaft. He was finding it hard work.

'At first examination it looks as if at one time it was a mine,' said Bergman. 'But I don't think it could have been that. Maybe at first but certainly not for some time. The galleries if any existed have all been sealed and that chamber with the bodies – most unusual.' He moved his boot over the soil, scraping at the dirt with its edge. It rose in a mound of fine particles to form a heap resembling ash.

'The inner lock of the door was broken,' Bergman mused. 'It must have been done deliberately which means that the creatures who sealed themselves in the chamber had no intention of ever leaving it. Perhaps they couldn't. Perhaps there was nowhere else they could go.' Again his boot scraped at the gritty soil. 'A last stand,' he said thoughtfully. 'The final retreat. Did they continue to hope, I wonder? Did some take their own lives? Or did they wait until their air escaped and died as they had lived in a common unity?'

'If they had lived that way.'

'They could live in no other, John. It took cooperation to work that metal, to form it, to set it into place. It took more to arrive at a common decision and to stick to it. To fashion the chamber and to enter it and wait. Perhaps they still had hope, John, but I doubt it. They would have seen too much, experienced too crushing a defeat for hope to have remained. And yet they must have had determination.' He paused then said, wistfully, 'I wished that we could have known them. There would have been much we could have learned and, towards the end at least, we'd have had much in common.'

The mutual necessity which had driven them to burrow deep into the ground, to construct tunnels, chambers, a means to survive. In that, at least, the aliens and the Alphans were alike. A common need and a common enemy. A common death, perhaps.

Koenig said, 'The beam?'

'It's obvious what it does, John. This is the final proof if we should need it. A force which weakens the molecular and atomic bonds and attracts the latent energy of matter itself. This planetoid could have been much larger than it is now. In fact I'm certain of it. The bodies we found proves that. There could have been an atmosphere, water, soil, growing things, villages, even. A small world but a pleasant one. Then it entered this space and was trapped by the Omphalos.'

Caught to be eaten by the beam as a boy would knaw at an apple on a stick. Matter reduced to energy and drawn away and, as the balance was altered the tiny world would have turned to expose a fresh portion of its surface to the devouring energy. Such a minute shift must have caused the closing of the door which had trapped Carter and Dale.

Koenig said, 'How fast, Victor?'

'Does the beam convert matter into energy? I don't know, John, we'll have to make tests to find out. But I don't think that it can be very fast. If the energy is liberated too quickly it could overload whatever mechanism or function the Omphalos uses to absorb it. And the people here had time to construct their tunnels.'

Digging like desperate rats to escape the inevitable. Delving deeper and deeper into their world as the surface was stripped away. Fighting to obtain a defence against premature aging, waiting, hoping, breeding, dying until, at the end, there was no more hope, nothing but extinction.

How long would it be until the Alphans reached that point?

How many generations? How many millenia? Ages? Eons?

And if they followed the same path would the final victims be even human?

'John?'

'I was thinking, Victor.'

'Of Alpha.' Bergman was shrewd. 'I know. The pattern is similar.'

The pattern, perhaps, but not necessarily the ingredients. The Alphans were human with all that implied. Born and reared against a background of ceaseless effort, their lives a continual act of violence, they had survived only because of all life-forms their planet had known they were the most ruthless.

Obeying a simple, savage creed.

To kill what they feared.

To destroy all that threatened.

Koenig said, 'Victor, when you've finished here return to base in Thomson's Eagle.'

'And you, John?'

'I'm going to visit the Omphalos.'

He travelled alone; if death waited there was no point in sharing the burden. The Eagle rose, leaving the planetoid behind as the engines sent it across space towards the pulsating green mass of the Omphalos. Koenig avoided the energy-beam, swinging around until he was at a point between the Moon and the remnant of what had once been a habitated world, then aimed the nose of the Eagle at its target.

'Commander?' Morrow stared from the screen. He blinked as Koenig gave his orders. 'A relay from Main Mission on upper register? Sure. I'll put it on the secondary channel. Two minutes.'

It appeared in one, the Omphalos a pale violet, the energy beams clear. Koenig looked at the image, comparing it with the direct view. On the relay his Eagle would be visible if Morrow increased the magnification, but he could do that only by narrowing the area of the visible field. It was better to scan a wider area – Koenig knew where he was.

'Commander?' Morrow was concerned. 'You're going in alone – how about some support?'

'No.'

'I could send more Eagles for rescue and as a backup and—'

'No, Paul!' Koenig snapped his impatience. 'I'm doing this alone. Watch the monitor but no support and no interference. Maintain continual check on all energy-fluctuations. Activate defence shield at low power and try to hit a bearable compromise between protection and power-loss. Understood?'

'Yes, Commander.'

'I'm making a reconnaissance,' said Koenig, more softly. 'Just a general probe to gather readings at close proximity. Victor should be with you soon but, until he arrives, you are in full command.'

He broke the connection, there was nothing more to say, nothing more to do now but wait as the engines killed the distance between the Eagle and its destination. Time to relax in the padded chair, to think, to speculate a little.

A brain.

Helena's analogy had been good and the likeness persisted even though he was seeing it from a different angle and from a closer point. The convoluted surface, the dark lines, the division between the hemispheres – all backed the similarity. But no brain could live without a body, a source of energy to maintain it, a skull to protect it. The thing could only be a mass of ordinary matter, barren, lifeless.

But, in that case, why did it pulsate?

An illusion? A trick of the light deceiving the eyes? Koenig narrowed his own watching, timing the apparent swell. Real or imagined? A thickening of the haze followed by a clarity would produce such a result. A gentle inflation and deflation the same. Even a steady rippling of the surface – but how could a solid mass ripple in such a manner?

He glanced at the upper register. The pale violet of the image was steadier than the normal view in green. The twin cones of pale luminescence seemed to drift over the surface as they followed the orbiting masses of the Moon and the planetoid.

Like hands, he thought, extended and grasping. Like the antennae of insects, the feelers of things which lived in darkness, the suckers of an octapod.

Koenig shook his head, irritated at his fantasies. He studied his instruments, seeing that the temperature of the Omphalos was still apparently zero despite the energy intake and its luminescence.

Well, soon now he might have the answer.

'Commander – you're getting close.'

Morrow on the screen with a warning Koenig could do without. He acknowledged it with a grunt then concentrated on sending the Eagle into a spiralling orbit around the pulsating central mass of this pocket universe.

Closer and he could see the convolutions now stark and clear. Not deep valleys as he had expected but gashes dulled with ebon tracery lying sombre and menacing in the twinkling haze. Closer still and beneath him the alien landscape spun towards the rear in a blur of mounds, dells, scoops, peaks, twistings, blurs, spinnings, whirlings, swirlings . . . windings . . . writhings . . .

Confusion which rose to engulf him.

'Koenig! John Koenig! You will hear me and you will obey!'

A voice echoing in his mind, verberating, booming as if from the far end of a long tunnel, amplified and empty, a remnant of the past.

'John Koenig you will succumb to my will. You are helpless to resist. You will obey . . . obey . . . obey . . .'

A school quadrangle, a gang, an elder boy confident of his physical strength, the loyalty of his sycophants. A spiritual weakling, a sadist, a vicious bully.

'John Koenig you will obey me without question. You will obey me in all things. You will obey!'

Now, as he had then, Koenig shouted his defiance.

'Go to hell!'

'What? You—'

'Go to hell!'

The voice was an illusion, a revived scrap of memory triggered by the hypnotic condition of the greenish illumination. It had to be that. Rock and stone and raw energy were not alive. Nothing could be alive in this seething hell.

Nothing – then why did he see a smiling face?

Pain stung the inside of his lip as his teeth met in the tender flesh. A stab of agony which cleared his eyes and banished the confusion so that he could clearly see the shape and position of the instruments before him, the controls of the Eagle in which he rode.

A switch which he closed.

'Paul!' he gasped. 'Paul, help me . . . help . . .'

A moment of clarity, gone almost as quickly as it had come, replaced by the swirling confusion which rose to take him and hurl him into chaos.

CHAPTER ELEVEN

He was a mote of life drifting in an endless, emerald sea. The waters were warm and comforting, lulling him with gentle surges, carrying him over a vast expanse of fretted stone and shells and strands of delicate weed. Other life drifted around him, small, innocent, scraps of awareness conscious only of the need to eat and to propagate, the sole pleasures of their limited existence.

When death came in a darting shadow of fin and jaw it was nothing.

Again he drifted, this time in an atmosphere of gentle breezes and solemn silences, the sun a shimmering orb of emerald splendour. Again he was minute but this time a little larger than before. A thinly constructed creature of vanes and sacs filled with hydrogen, of foils to catch and use the wind, of muscles to bunch and make dense his bodily substance so that, at will, he could gain height or lose it, could drift with the wind or tack against it.

He and the uncountable numbers of others who hung with him in the emerald sky.

Food for larger beings of more complex structure. Drifting giants who roved the atmosphere and browsed on the clouds of things of which he was a single part.

And again, when death came, it was nothing.

Death was always nothing.

The gateway to a new existence, a door which all things had to use, a path every living creature had to take. Death was not an ending but a new beginning. The old cells and structure broken, torn into their component parts, incorporated into other, more sophisticated arrangements. The pattern of the mind released from its fleshly bonds to free the spirit which would pass on to join the single great accumulation of all feeling, all experience, all knowledge, all awareness, all consciousness which was the gestalt of the universe.

And it was right that the larger should feed on the smaller, the lesser give its awareness and substance to a thing of greater complexity. As atoms had been created in the empty space to form molecules and compounds and thus the basic matter of planets and suns so the single-celled gave to the many-celled and they, in turn, gave to those higher in the evolutionary scale.

The way of life and the arrow of time.

The ladder which reached from primeval mud to the stars.

The sacrifice which gave the ultimate peace.

Peace.

'No!' Koenig stirred, something within him rebelling, waking, protesting. 'No!'

'Such foolishness,' whispered a thin voice. 'Such stupidity. What are a few days when set against the total span of time? What is a lifetime when set against eternity?'

'No, damn you! No!'

'Why fight, John Koenig? Why continue to carry the burden? You've carried it long enough and there will be no end to the weight, the responsibility, the guilt. You killed Frank Dale. You killed Tony Ellman. You killed Ivor Khokol. You killed . . . you killed . . . you killed . . .'

The list of names seemed endless.

The guilt a burden on his soul.

Each who had died and who would die was his concern. He was the commander, his the decision and therefore his the responsibility. Always his was the responsibility. Always his would be the guilt.

Always.

'No,' he said, stubbornly. 'It isn't like that.'

'But it is, John Koenig,' whispered the voice. 'It always has been. It always will be. How many can you order to their deaths? How long can you rest hearing their cries and reproaches? One mistake and all will die. One mistake . . . one . . . only one . . .'

Once dead he would be freed from the possibility that he would make that mistake.

'No,' he said, again. 'No.'

The voice was a lie. It was the sound of cowardice, the lure of timidity. Yield, give up, cease the struggle and be rewarded with eternal regret. A bribe which had no substance.

Who was tempting him?

Who – or *what*?

A red eye began to blink at him, flash . . flash . . . flash . . . A cyclops which demanded attention. Koenig stared at it, seeing it through a green haze, a swirl of distorted reality. It was hard to concentrate. It would be easier simply to lean back and relax and to close his eyes and to sink into that wonderful state of utter detachment in which nothing had importance and nothing really mattered because, in the end, all things would be the same.

So easy to lean back . . . to drift . . . to drift . . .

Paul Morrow scowled at his instruments, the expression accentuating the lines on his face, a fatigue. A deep, bone-nagging weariness aggravated by his frustration.

'Nothing.' He checked a row of instruments, fingers stabbing at buttons, cross-meshing circuits. From the consol little lamps flared, tell-tales merging with illuminated dials and digital readouts, monitors which told him the condition of every sector of the base. 'Nothing,' he said again. 'The Eagle's dead.'

'Keep trying.' Victor Bergman studied the screens, the images they carried. 'Keep trying, Paul.'

'I'm sending out a continuous signal but there's no answer. I've tried to use the override but there's no response. Something is cancelling out the signals and I can't gain remote control. Try, you say, I've tried everything I know.' His voice rose a little grew bitter. 'Damn it, Professor! Do you think I've just been sitting here twiddling my thumbs?'

'No, Paul, of course not.' Fatigue bred short tempers, but as Bergman knew Morrow's outburst was less due to weariness than to a stronger feeling. He, like all of them, was sick with worry and concern for the lone man in the distant Eagle.

'He hasn't landed,' said Morrow quietly. 'He's orbiting the Omphalos but so close he must be skimming the edge of any force field it might have. Field or atmosphere,' he added, bleakly. 'God alone knows what he's found out there.'

'Sandra?'

'No change, Professor. I've been monitoring the path of the Commander's flight pattern and there is no discernable energy-variation.'

'Which means that he can hardly be cutting through a force field if one should exist,' mused Bergman. 'If he was we'd surely spot a halation.'

'Only if the situation out there followed a familiar electronic sequence.' Sandra checked her instruments again. 'Surface temperature still zero. No measurable radiation. No magnetic flux. There seems to be no reason why the Commander just can't level orbit and head back to Alpha.'

'Paul?'

'His guidance systems could be frozen in some way. I've sent out checking signals and received no response but that could be due to a different cause.' Morrow shook his head, baffled. 'He's out there. We know it and know just where to find him. As far as I can determine all systems are operational.'

'So?'

'Either the Commander has deliberately cut the remotes or they have failed to function because of some local effect. The Omphalos could be surrounded with a blanket of electronic distortion which traps all emissions. That could explain why I'm getting no personal contact.'

'But surely the Commander would know that and return?' Sandra Benes, well-versed in survival disciplines, knew the regular safety-procedure. 'He wouldn't risk his life and an Eagle for nothing.'

Bergman said, 'Perhaps he has no choice.'

'Professor?'

'He could be unconscious or hurt in some way. It is the only explanation for his continued radio silence unless the Omphalos has a distortion field as Paul suggests. At this very moment the Commander could be calling on us for help.' Bergman frowned at the screens. 'Paul, is an energy-cone impinging on the Eagle?'

'No.'

Another mystery – why cones on the Moon and the planetoid

and not on the Eagle? The mass too small, perhaps? The object too near?

Questions which could wait – but one problem could not.

'Kano, have you checked the rate of descent? How much time do we have before the Eagle crashes?'

From where he stood beside the computer David Kano said, 'What's on your mind, Professor? Rescue?'

'Is it possible?'

Kano fed the problem into the machine and tore the slip from the readout.

Morrow saw him frown. 'What's wrong, David?'

'A moment.' Again Kano busied himself with the computer, made a check, looked up from the final result. 'A new factor has been added,' he said, bleakly. 'The rate of orbital decay is accelerating faster than it should. Either something has slowed the Eagle or it is being affected by a force from below.'

'Well?'

'At the present velocity and with the decay remaining as plotted we have time to reach the Eagle and have approximately, ten minutes in which to effect an exchange and escape.'

Ten minutes!

It would have to be enough.

Alan Carter sat in the pilot's chair. He had heard the news and had risen from his hospital bed and had insisted on his right to command the rescue ship. A right backed by his unquestionable skill.

'You'll need the best,' he said. 'I'm the best. I've the training and the experience and if I can't do it no one can. Not a boast, Professor, a fact and you know it.'

'But are you fit?'

'I'm fit.' Carter had shrugged. 'So I lost my breath for a while but I've got it back now. I've had plenty of time to regain it and I'll have more on the journey out. David can pilot the Eagle until we reach the Omphalos.' He added, impatiently, 'Let's not argue about it – we haven't time for that.'

But time had been found to install a few items of equipment

Bergman had selected. Time too for Helena Russell to bring aboard things of her own.

Like Alan Carter she had insisted on accompanying the rescue mission and, like Carter, she was not to be denied.

Now she busied herself in the passenger module, mixing fluids, sealing small containers, fastening them to pipes leading to masks which could be clipped over the mouth and nostrils. Standard equipment which Bergman recognised as being parts of emergency resuscitation apparatus.

'Here, Victor.' She handed him one. 'Loop this over your head and drop the container into your suit. Wear the mask or leave it to rest just below your mouth. There's a valve here, see? Turn it if you feel odd in any way.'

'Such as?'

'Giddiness, detachment, disorientation.'

'You expect such reactions?'

'I don't know what to expect, Victor, but I'm trying to anticipate. John wouldn't just freeze unless he had no choice. The Eagle is protected against most things and if the trouble is other than physical what I've built won't help much. The flasks contain an anti-hallucinogen in liquid form under pressure. Turning the valve will release a fine spray which will turn into a vapour. It will do much as the capsules I made before we hit this space. If we are subjected to sensory distortion or cerebral stimulation then the gas could help.'

'How? As a depressant?' Bergman was interested. Adjusting the device he twisted the valve and took a cautius sniff. 'It smells like ammonia.'

'A scent incorporated as a warning that the valve is open,' she explained. 'Also it serves to tighten the inner membranes and clear the nasal passages so as to allow an easy entry of the vapour into the lungs. The chemical formulae is complex, an extension of what I used before.' She added, sombrely, 'I hope that it can help.'

As Bergman hoped that his own devices would work.

As Helena rose to carry other containers of the anti-hallucinogen to where Kano and Carter sat in the pilot's seats of the Eagle he stooped over the apparatus he had brought with him. It was a jumble of electronic circuits, radiant coils, batteries, vibrators, crystals and other assorted pieces of electronic equipment snatched from his laboratory. Now he connected parts to each other, fed power into the assembly, watched as dials kicked and registers glowed.

Returning Helena watched him, saw his frown, his irritable shake of the head.

'Trouble, Victor?'

'Yes.'

'What is it?'

'Something I've been working on. A compact form of a heterodying apparatus which I intend to fit to the regular screen installations of the Eagles. As you know there are two ways at least of gaining protection from energies which may threaten to disrupt or damage life and equipment. We can prevent it reaching us – in other words set up a barrier of some kind which is stronger than the threatening energy, or we can diffuse it. Our present defence shield works on the former principle. We set up an umbrella of controlled energy, held and directed by powerful fields which is strong enough to prevent the passage of inimical forces. It also helps to diffuse the energy by forcing it to spread its point of impact so that no one point is subjected to the total.'

'Like a shield of steel fronted by a layer of fluid,' she said. 'The fluid spreads the impact and the steel stops it. I understand.'

'Such a system requires weight and a plentiful supply of power.' Bergman made another adjustment and grunted as a lamp flashed. 'I'm trying to do something different.'

'Heterodying,' she said. 'Cancelling out. One force merging with and diminishing another. I remember an experiment conducted in the science lab when I was at school. Two different sounds which were blended to result in silence. Two lamps the same. As I remember it the crests of one wave-form had to match exactly with the valleys of another. By combining the two you ended with a total cancellation of both.'

'Yes.' Bergman moved a connection. 'What I hope to do is to build a field, even a minor one will do, around this Eagle so that whatever force is affecting John's vessel won't affect us.'

'You think it important?'

He said, flatly, 'John is no fool, Helena. He isn't maintaining radio silence because he wants to. And his controls aren't jammed from choice. He's trapped and something has trapped him. Both of us have recognised that.'

And recognised, too, that they in turn could be rendered as helpless as the commander. Doomed, as Koenig was doomed, to circle the Omphalos until their Eagle crashed to destructive ruin.

And, for them, there would be no rescue.

From his chair Kano said, 'We're getting close. You want to take over now?'

'Not yet, David.' Alan Carter stared through the forward vision ports, narrowing his eyes against the green glow of the Omphalos, trying to see the minute shape of the Eagle against the convoluted mass. Before him an instrument clicked, clicked again, took up a repetitious buzzing.

'Got it!' Kano stared at his own bank of instruments. 'The tracer has hooked on to the Commander's Eagle. Distance . . . velocity . . . direction . . .' He read out the figures even as he was turning their own machine into a complementary path to the other. 'If you're ready I'll—' He broke off, blinking. 'What's that? What the hell is it?'

Something huge, monstrous, rising on wings of lambent flame, eyes like mirrors of ice, jaws gaping wide enough to swallow them whole.

'The laser! Quick!' Kano cried out as the thing engulfed them, seeing darkness as his senses swam and a giddiness turned his limbs to water. Dead, swallowed, made one with the great flying beast – the creature from nightmare. Why hadn't Carter fired? Why had he let them be killed?

'David!' He heard the voice as from a great distance. 'David! Get hold of yourself, man! David!'

Kano shuddered, seeing again the terrible shape of the Mbolnga bird, the frightful avenger which came to tear the living hearts from the guilty, to gulp down those who had run from battle and hold them in its stomach there to be pulped to a living, screaming jelly. Old tales whispered to his great-grandfather in the flickering light of camp fires, murmurs from reeded kralls, hints given by the witch doctors with their devils masks and mysterious powers.

How deep ran the racial heritage of mankind!

'David!' Carter was anxious, his voice betraying his rising anger. David, for God's sake, man!'

Kano said, dully, 'Didn't you see it?'

'See what?'

'A great bird. It came from nothing and—' He broke off, realising that it was useless to explain. The thing had vanished as quickly as it had come. 'Are we still tracking?'

'Yes.' Carter checked the instruments with a practiced sweep of his eyes. 'That bird you thought you saw. Was it—'

'Not thought,' said Kano. 'I did see it. To me, at least, it was real.'

'All right. That bird you saw. Did it . . .' Alan blinked. In the co-pilot's seat a skeleton sat, grinning at him, hollow sockets controls, taking over from his co-pilot, the terrible figure which moved as the head turned, the fleshless jaws gaping in the ghastly parody of a smile.

Death as his companion.

Death in the Eagle.

Death at his side!

Tell-tales flared and alarms sounded as Carter tore at the controls, taking over from his co-pilot, the terrible figure which sat in menace at his side. Around him swirled a thin, green mist, blurring details, softening harsh outlines, seeming to cling to hands and head, face and hair, filling his lungs, thickening, solidifying, clogging . . . clogging . . .

And, abruptly, he was back in the sealed chamber where the aliens had died. His suit closed, the air gone, the enclosed space filled with the taint of his own vomit. He felt again the sickening heaving of his lungs and stomach, the desperate need for air, to breathe, to escape.

And death, as before, was waiting.

Death with its quiet and subtle peace.

The warm and gentle darkness into which he could sink and rest . . . and rest . . . and rest . . .

As Kano fought for their lives.

Carter had taken over full control and then had seemingly gone to sleep. Kano slapped at the switches, overrode the máster control and regained command. Beneath his hands the Eagle was a horse running wild, a ship in a storm, a leaf riding a whirlpool. Lamps flashed their signals of overstrained systems; guidance mechanisms fought opposing impulses, the stabilizers were at war with themselves, the engines were blasting against a reverse thrust, even the life-support systems were flashing in the red.

Within moments circuits would blow as feed-back current fused resistances and jumped gaps never intended to handle such misapplied energies.

'David, your mask!' He heard Helena shout. 'The mask. Both of you use the mask!'

She was standing in the door leading back to the passenger module, her face pale, a smear of blood running over her chin from a bitten lip. A moment then she had vanished, flung backwards by the abrupt movement of the Eagle; a sudden acceleration which drove Kano deep into his chair and sent sparks flashing before his eyes.

Another illusion or reality?

How could he tell?

He groaned, fighting the pressure, tasting blood as his hand moved up towards the mask hanging below his mouth. The valve seemed to be stuck, the knob rejecting his fingers and he groaned again as, with added desperation, he again attacked the metal. A year and the valve moved a little. A century and it opened a little more. A mellenia and he smelt the stink of ammonia which rose to burn in his nostrils, to tingle in his lungs.

To wash his brain free of fantasy and to reveal the peril ahead.

The Eagle was plunging to utter destruction.

'Alan!' Kano yelled as he fought the controls. He was a good pilot, trained, normally capable, but if the Eagle were to be saved now they wanted not mere capability but a miracle. 'Alan, for God's sake!'

Before his eyes the signal lamps flared like the dancing of dust flecks on a stove. In the forward vision ports the bulk of the Omphalos shone with a hungry, green glow, filling the area, the shadowed convolutions taking on the likeness of a mask, a grinning face, a waiting skull.

They were heading towards it too fast and at too steep an angle. Already they must be below the orbit followed by the other Eagle. If dangerous fields were present they had already entered them, to escape, would require skills perfected beyond the hampering need of thought. Carter had them, Kano knew he did not.

Freezing the controls he lunged towards the other man, gripped the valve of his mask, opened it, fell back into his seat just in time to prevent the Eagle going into a long-axis rotating spin.

'What?' Carter stirred. 'What's the matter? What happened – Kano!'

'Take over, man! You wanted to come. You said you were the best and, now's your chance to prove it. Wake up, man!'

'I'm awake.'

'Then take over.' Kano hit a switch and folded his arms. 'Here! It's all yours. Now show us how good you are!'

There was nothing more he could do now but pray.

CHAPTER TWELVE

Once, when he had been very young, Victor Bergman had been taken by an uncle to a far land and there, at an ancient and holy place, had paid a coin to a fakir who had asked him what most he wanted to be. The man had smiled when he had answered and had gently corrected the youthful aspirations. It was not enough, he said, to be rich and wise and famous. It was not even enough for a man to be clever. Above all a man, any man, needed to be lucky.

Now, sitting in the Eagle, Bergman realised again that, not for the first time, his luck had saved his life.

Against all odds Carter had managed to regain control. Against all logic the jumble of equipment he had assembled had, by sheer chance, formed connections which had produced the heterodyning field he had hoped would give protection. And Helena's compound had saved them from mind-destroying hallucinations.

Hunched in his seat he brooded over the stream of images, the false reality in which, for a space, he had been lost.

A vision of plumed horses, of crepe and solemn black, of mournful faces and mutes and bearers and arm-bands and hats dressed with ebon ribbons. All the pomp and planopy of a Victorian funeral. The exaggerated respect paid to the dead with doffed caps and bowed heads, of whispering voices, of ceremonial meals.

Of mourning extended.

Of grief maintained.

It was in his mind, all of it, memories and facts gathered when a boy, of the weight of the customs of the time, of the heritage from which he had come. The mystique of death, caught, transported, used as a weapon against him, directed by his own subconscious so as to resemble a haven of peace.

And Helena?

She had been more wary than he, opening her valve before

succumbing to the illusions, warned by her medical skill, sensitive to little signs of which he would have been unaware. A distortion of the light, perhaps, a slowness of thought or co-ordination.

'It worked,' he said. 'We've found a way to beat the Omphalos.'

'Perhaps.' She did not share his conviction. 'A medical trick, Victor, but we can't continue to inhale drugs. Unless we discontinue their use soon the balance will have swung the other way and the anti-hallucinogens will produce distorting side effects.'

'Such as?' He didn't really want to know. 'Never mind. As soon as we collect John we can get away from here. When will that be?'

Alan alone had the answer. As Bergman and Helena entered the command module he said, without turning in his chair, 'We're now in orbit following a path a little higher than the other Eagle. We've resestablished the tracking monitor and have course and direction plotted. All that remains now is to go in.'

'When?'

'It has to be soon. I'd like to take a few minutes to confirm relative courses and to establish any local patterns of variable turbulance. There could be magnetic fields, eddy-currents, areas of constrasting potential.'

'We didn't find any,' reminded Bergman. 'All sensors registered negative.'

'They still do.' Carter made a slight adjustment. 'But I'd like to be sure. As it is we won't have the chance.'

The time factor, of course, Bergman had almost forgotten it. 'We have ten minutes,' he said.

'We had.' Carter was grim. 'We haven't now. We used it up regaining control. You can give David the thanks for that,' he added. 'If it hadn't been for him we'd all be dead now. If he ever gets tired of nursing his machine he can transfer to Reconnaissance any time he wants.'

From Carter that was high praise and Kano beamed his gratification. But nothing, they all knew, would ever woo him away from the one great love of his life. To him the computer was more than a machine. It was an actual, living creature.

And one with a mellifluous woman's voice.

'Is that John's Eagle?' Helena leaned forward as a fleck appeared on the screen. 'There!'

It grew as they watched it, taking on shape and substance, a a little vague against the greenish glow, the bulk of the Omphalos into which it was heading.

'Still no contact?'

'No, Professor.' Kano checked his instruments. 'We should be able to reach him but he doesn't answer.' He added, 'And no contact with Alpha.'

As Bergman had expected. His own heterodying field which maintained the Eagle's systems from interference would also bolster the radio-barrier.

'We're going in,' said Carter. 'Get ready for the exchange. We'll have no time to waste so make it fast. Kano?'

'Four minutes total starting from – now!'

Four minutes in which to make actual physical contact with the other Eagle, to establish the seal, to enter and to carry Koenig back to safety. Bergman felt the deck of the Eagle move beneath his feet as he sealed his helmet. Helena had done the same and he stepped to where she was standing before the hatch and, counting seconds, waited.

Forty-three and the Eagle dipped, veered, juddered as Carter fought to bring it into alignment with the other vessel.

'Sixty-two and the clash of touching metal rang through the hull.

Eighty-seven and again the hulls touched, parted, touched again, the hulls clamped with the air of powerful electromagnets.

'Contact!' Carter signalled to Kano. 'Establish and hold. Professor! Get moving!'

Two minutes in which to pass through the hatches, enter the other Eagle, get Koenig, return, seal, break apart and head away from the nearing danger of the Omphalos.

Bergman went first, slamming open the port, reaching for the other with barely a glance at the enclosing seal of transparent, flexible plastic which joined the hulls together like a fat section of hose. The external lock resisted his tug and he threw his weight against it, conscious of the passing seconds.

'Hurry, Victor!' Helena's voice was strained. Tense as it came from his phones. 'Hurry!'

The lock yielded, the port opened and Bergman thrust himself into the command module of Koenig's Eagle. The commander was slumped in his chair before the controls, head forward, face hidden by the fold of his arms.

'One minute!' said Carter. 'Hurry!'

'Get back in the Eagle, Helena,' snapped Bergman, as she stepped towards the figure in the pilot's chair. 'There's no time for you to treat him now. Get back and clear the way.'

'He could be hurt! Lifting him wrongly could kill him!'

A gamble they would all have to take. As she stepped back Bergman moved to the chair, stooped, thrust his arms beneath the limp form and lifted. Koenig sagged, one arm falling to trail across the back of the seat, his head almost hitting the edge of the port as Bergman passed through it. Helena slammed it shut.

'Twelve seconds!' Carter's voice was brittle with tension. 'Have you got him safe?'

'Safe,' said Bergman.

'Good! Kano break seal. Stand by for emergency lift. Now!'

The note of the engines rose, became a throbbing roar, exhaust gases blasting from the venturis as the Eagle tore free from the other vessel and began to lift from the danger below. For a moment it seemed as if they had waited too long, taken one chance too many, then, with a gusting sigh of relief, Kano saw the movement of needles, the shift of perspective.

'We've done it! Man, we've done it!'

Carter relaxed a little as the greenish bulk of the Omphalos dropped away. Against it the shape of the other vessel grew small, almost vanished, then suddenly expended in an eye searing patch of raw and crimson flame.

'Three seconds,' said Kano. 'Three seconds more and we'd have shared that pyre.' He shuddered then said, without turning, 'How is the commander?'

He was lying where Bergman had placed him, face down, arms hiding his cheeks, his knees bent a little. He looked a man asleep; only the steady rise and fall of his chest showing that he was still alive. Helena knelt and gently turned him over.

Bergman heard the sharp sound of her indrawn breath.

'Helena?'

'His face,' she whispered. 'Dear God, look at his face!'

It was old with an oldness which went beyond mere attrition of tissues. The lines were too deep, the skin too taut, the creped patches wide-spread so that he looked as a withered mummy might look or a corpse which had been left to desiccate in some tropic sun.

'John!' Helena threw back her helmet and stooped over him, her eyes wet with tears. 'John!'

A call to the man she had known, the person with whom she had shared a fantastic adventure and perhaps a little more than that. Bergman saw her shoulders move in the unmistakable signs of grief and stood, feeling a little helpless, a little unwanted.

And, he too felt grief.

They had wanted a miracle and for a brief moment he had thought that one had been granted. The Eagle contacted, the hallucinations banished, the crippling stress-fields cancelled out and the commander saved. But saved for what?

'He's dying!' said Helena. 'Dying!'

Cursed by the age-accelerator which threatened the base. The sucking beam which drew life and energy from all it touched. Ellman had died because of it and, even now, others might have succumbed.

But no beam had impinged on the Eagle.

Bergman said, 'Helena. It might not be what you think. The vapour – quickly!'

'This isn't an hallucination, Victor.'

'To us, no, but to John?' He left the question hanging. 'Try the vapour. Try it!'

Koenig coughed as she stripped the apparatus from around

her neck and held the mask to his mouth and nose. He stirred, one hand lifted as, weakly, he tried to push the device away.

'It isn't going to work,' she said, dully. 'We've rescued him only to watch him die.'

Of senility, spending his last few days or hours like a crippled animal, his mind gone, his strength, his agility.

It would have been better to have left him to burn in the pyre of the fallen Eagle.

A quick and merciful death.

'Helena!' Bergman leaned forward from where he stood. 'It's working. Look!'

Koenig's face changed. The creped and desiccated skin began to smooth, the lines to fill, the corpse-like appearance to vanish. Dark circles remained around his eyes and his face still bore traces of age, but they were the result of fatigue, of muscles strained and settled into a mask of exhaustion.

'John!' Helena caught him as he coughed again and tried to stir. His cheeks, Bergman noted, were moist with her tears. 'John! Oh, John!'

His eyes opened and he stared at her with a blank expression. A man in a daze, unbelieving that what he saw could be real. One who tried to smile and gasped and sucked vapour into his lungs and who, as they watched, became the man they had known and respected.

'Helena.' Bergman dropped his hand to her shoulder. 'He'll be all right now. Just give him time to recover.'

And to give herself time to gain composure, to adopt once more the iron mask of professional detachment.

But she could not forget what she had seen; the apparent miracle which had turned an old and dying man into one little older than herself and obviously fit.

'The vapour,' she said. 'It had to be that. But how did you know it would work?'

'I didn't,' he confessed. 'But now it seems obvious what must have happened. John was alone, unprotected, the victim of God knows what hallucinations. We both know the power of illusion; under hypnosis a man can be convinced he cannot walk and he will be a literal cripple. Hysterical blindness, paralysis, loss of taste, smell, and touch – you must have seen many cases.'

'I have,' she admitted then added slowly, 'So you are saying that John was suffering from a psychosomatic condition?'

'What else?' Bergman paused, remembering his own experience. 'He must have been subjected to intensely strong hallucinations formed of age and death, decay and collapse. Hallucinations so strong that they became an integral part of him and affected his actual physical being. Once convince the mind of a thing and the body will follow. Drench it with the concept of age and the facial muscles will respond; the skin alter texture, the capillaries enlarge, the tissue show all the signs of desiccation. But, Helena, as a doctor you know all this.'

She had known it, but had been too disturbed to look beyond the obvious. Bergman had done that, his mind relatively free of the emotions which had numbed her. The attribute of his mechanical heart, perhaps, or—

She shook her head, annoyed with the vein of calculation. What did it matter how he had arrived at the conclusion he had? His suggestion had worked and Koenig was himself again.

He smiled as, again, she leaned over him.

'Helena! Are you real?'

'Yes, John. I'm real.'

'You came after me,' he said, slowly. 'Rescued me.' His eyes moved from the woman to where Bergman stood silently watching. 'You and Victor and who else?' He frowned as she told him. 'And what if you had been trapped as I was?'

'Nothing.' She met his eyes. 'Victor left orders that under no circumstances was a second rescue attempt to be made.'

She, all of them, had taken a calculated gamble with death but there was nothing he could say. The decision had been a personal one and he would have done exactly the same. One attempt could be justified – more could not. Alpha could not afford to waste crews and Eagles.

As he climbed to his feet to stand, unsteadily, one hand supporting his weight, Bergman said, 'You were locked in orbit around the Omphalos, John. You had time to study it. Did you—'

'Decide what it was?' Koenig shrugged. 'I only know one thing, Victor. It is inimical – and it is alive.'

Alive in a way in which nothing in his experience had been alive. A node of awareness, self-contained, a mesh of balanced energies forming a living, conscious world. And it was conscious, of that he had no doubt. Sitting in the passenger compartment of the Eagle, eyes half-closed, he recalled and relived that dreadful time during which the entire universe had been filled with the desire and the concept of death.

'It's sentient,' he explained. 'A form of life which we can only understand by analogy. Think of an oyster or a barnacle. A plant such as a Venus Flytrap. A sea-urchin, a leech, a basking whale. The Omphalos is all of these and more. You called it a brain, Helena. It is that too.'

'A conscious brain?' Bergman was fast with the question. 'Are the beams directed against the Moon and the planetoid the result of a conscious decision?'

'Intelligent direction, John?' Helena frowned. 'Is it possible?'

He said, dully, conscious of the inability of mere words to convey what he had felt and emotionally comprehend, 'Perhaps not intelligent as we use the term. Those beams could have been emitted as we would put out a hand to touch something. Or as a parasite would automatically introduce a proboscis into the skin of a victim. It reacted to our presence. Perhaps it couldn't help but to react. It, like ourselves, like all living things, is driven by the need to survive. To it we are little more than a source of energy.'

Food!

Helena looked at where the Omphalos was pictured on a screen to the fore of the compartment. It was smaller now they were on their way back to Alpha. Carter, she noticed had, with innate caution, taken a flight path which kept them well clear of the energy-sucking cone.

Even as she watched the green expanse seemed to flex with its mysterious pulsations.

A creature born in an alien dimension stirring at the impact of intelligent life?

Responding to mental stimuli received, perhaps, at a paraphysical level?

And if the thing were sleeping and should wake – what then?

The concept chilled her then she shook herself, aware of her flight into fantasy, the sudden flurry of an undisciplined imagination. It was a relief to listen to what Bergman was saying.

'John, you said that to the Omphalos we were little more than a source of energy. That is a source of food. Do you imply that we could be even more?'

A moment in which Koenig remained silent, looking ahead with haunted eyes, aware of the trap into which his private knowledge had led him. The impression he had gained of something into which other sentient creatures could and had been assimilated. Of a plethora of minds aware and helplessly entrammelled. Of the ghostly echoes of screams.

'Perhaps,' he said at last. And then, to change the subject, 'Did you manage to measure the rate of attrition on the planetoid?'

'Not to the precision I would like, John, but we took some rough measurements. It is slow as I anticipated. We seem to be dealing with a total conversion of matter into energy and there must be a limiting factor to the amount which can be stored and utilised.' He added, grimly. 'But there's no danger of the thing going hungry for a long time yet. The mass of the Moon alone will keep it supplied for millennia.'

The rock, the dust and stone. The minerals and chemicals and deposits. The people too, but Koenig didn't want to think of that.

Helen pressed him back in the seat as he attempted to rise.

'Take it easy, John. There's nothing for you to do now.'

'I want to see if we can contact the base.'

'Why?' She frowned as he made no answer. 'The defence shield? Paul kept it on as you ordered. Anything else?'

'The metal we found,' he said. 'The olive stuff lining the tunnels and chamber of the aliens. Did you find out what it was, Victor?'

'Basically some form of non-ferrous alloy aligned to long-chain polymers of a silicone structure. They must have found a way to blend the various materials into a flux which they spread and let harden as we do with an epoxy glue. Once set it's difficult to cut and impossible to rework.'

'Can we duplicate it?'

'Not at the moment and I doubt if we will ever be able to match it exactly.' Bergman rubbed thoughtfully at his chin. 'I didn't have much time to work on it myself, but Zakym Allivare is doing his best. He knows metals and plastics better than any, John. If there's an answer to be found then he'll find it.'

Koenig nodded, remembering the man, a solemn, middle-aged product of the Levant, a person who rarely smiled but had never, to his knowledge, displayed anger.

Helena said, 'Why the interest, John? What importance can the alien metal have for us?'

'Those creatures used it for protection,' he explained. 'They lined their tunnels and chamber with it.'

'Naturally, so as to seal them against air-loss.' She saw his eyes, his expression. 'But you think there was something else, John. A protection against what?' Her mind leapt to the answer. 'The aging element of the energy-beam? Is that it?'

'I don't know. It was only a possibility.'

'We could make a test.' Helena frowned, thinking. 'Culture plates,' she decided. 'Bob is already working with them and Allivare could shield them with some of the alien metal and see if there is any change in the katabolic rate.'

'See if the radio is working. If it is give the orders.'

Koenig tried to relax as she left, knowing there was nothing more he could do for the present. If contact could be established then everything possible for the moment would have been done.

In the meantime it was good just to sit, to know that he was safe among his fellows, that the ghastly isolation he had known when orbiting the Omphalos was a thing of the past.

Something to be forgotten – if such a thing could ever be that.

'John!' He started and opened his eyes aware that he must have dosed. Helena was beside him.

'Did you get through?'

'Finally, yes.'

'And?'

She said, flatly, 'Zakym Allivare is dead.'

CHAPTER THIRTEEN

He had died as Tony Ellman had died, falling to lie in his suit, suffering from terminal senility, dead of old age before he could be rescued from the site on which he had chosen to work.

'I warned him,' said Mathias. 'I told him of the danger and begged him to use remote control apparatus but he wouldn't listen. He just wanted to work and forget.' He added, as if in explanation, 'He left a wife and two young children back on earth.'

Koenig said, 'Was he on the right track? Can the alien metal give protection?'

'No.' Mathias picked up a folder and checked the notations. 'Do you want the details? Over a grand total of twenty-three tests the figures are—'

'Never mind the figures, Bob. In your opinion to continue working with the metal for that object is to waste time. Right?'

Mathias nodded. 'Yes, Commander. If the aliens used it to block the aging process then their metabolism must have been far different from our own.'

Helena said, 'Are there any other casualties, Bob?'

'Two, neither fatal.' He gestured towards the intensive care unit. 'Nyat Cheng and Brad Marshall. Both outside workers.'

'Treatment?'

'Complete blood-changes, massive injections of hormones, drips of saline and glucose, marrow-implants to restore red-corpuscle production, anti-calcium treatment and wide-range antibiotics injected at frequent intervals.' Mathias made a helpless gesture. 'I don't think anything we can try will work. If it did we'd have made an advance in geriactics. The most we can hope for is to stave off the inevitable.'

To give a little more life, a greater extension which needn't be the benefit it seemed. Had Nyat Cheng also lost a wife and children? Had Brad Marshall? Were they, like Zakym Allivare, the victims of an unconscious urge to commit suicide?

Or were they no more than the victims of carelessness?

'There is to be no further work on the surface,' said Koenig. 'All personnel restricted to base and all unessential workers to be kept confined to the lower levels. Those working close to the outside to be rotated at frequent intervals.' He snatched the commlock from his belt. 'Victor?'

Bergman stared from the tiny screen.

'What is it, John?'

'An emergency conference in my office in ten minutes. Bring all available data on the present situation with special emphasis on the rate of energy flow from targets to main body.' Koenig pressed a button. 'Channon?'

'Here, Commander.'

'Adjust all atomic piles to the maximum production of plutonium.'

'All?' The atomic engineer looked startled. 'Remember the storage problems, Commander.'

'All,' said Koenig. 'Use automatics and take risks with the non-essential equipment if you must, but I want top-production.'

As he pressed another button Helena said, 'What's in your mind, John?'

'Survival.'

'By producing plutonium?' She blinked as, ignoring the question, he relayed a stream of orders to other sections of the base. 'John! What are you doing?'

'Come to the conference,' he snapped. 'And find out.'

It was a meeting dominated by one man and she realised that, subconsciously, he had made his decision long before taking his place behind his wide desk. The doors were closed but, beyond, in Main Mission, the instruments were watching their common enemy. The green, brain-like mass of the Omphalos. The enigmatic thing which held them trapped, was sucking away energy and life, which had to be destroyed.

As Koenig emphasised the point she realised that she had expected it. Had even accepted it.

Bergman alone was dubious.

'If, as you say, it has rudimentary awareness, John, then

destroying it without regard would be in the nature of an immoral act. Have we the right to use violence? Must life always be gained at the expense of another's?'

Koenig said, slowly, 'Victor, we have no choice. 'Men are dead and dying because of it. The aliens were wiped out. No one knows how many other life-forms and races have been destroyed by that thing. It is killing us and, to save ourselves, we must render it harmless. I am willing to listen to any other feasible alternative. You have one?'

'Can we communicate with it in some way?' Channon of atomics ran his hand through his thinning hair. 'Have we tried?'

'Yes.'

'Without success?'

'I've been in touch with it as close as I believe any intelligent creature can be.' Koenig's face hardened as he remembered the seeming eternity of loneliness, the numbing pressure of all things associated with death, the deaths he had mentally experienced, the hunger he had sensed, the ferocity. 'I don't know if we can call it alive as we use the term, perhaps it is nothing more than a reactive device, the result of an experiment, perhaps, something which lies beyond our knowledge and previous experience. But I do know, and know it with every fibre of my being, that unless we destroy it it will destroy us. To me the choice is simple, Victor?'

'As you say, John.'

'Helena?'

'I agree.'

Channon said, before he was asked. 'The safety of Alpha comes first, Commander – but can we destroy it? Can we even hurt it?'

'I think we can.' Koenig glanced at Bergman. 'You have the figures, Victor. We know the energy potential available to us. If we use it correctly we have a chance.' He ended, bleakly, 'It's the only one we have.'

Alan Carter had been the first to volunteer. Now he sat at the controls of the Eagle on the launching pad watching the brilliant display in his screens. The defence shield arching over him was a dome of scintillant rainbows, sparkling, coruscating, heart-stoppingly beautiful. It would, he hoped, protect him from becoming prematurely old. Bergman had said that it would, that the balance of energies now achieved would, at least, stave off the fate suffered by Ellman and Allivare. That he would not end on a cot as Cheng and Marshall had done and now they too were dead and three others had taken their place.

The last, he hoped and had justification. They had worked on the surface. Since the ban no other cases had been reported.

'Ready, Alan?'

Paul Morrow talking from the screen. Carter nodded then said, 'Ready when you are.'

'Right. On five. Mark!' His voice held no expression as he gave the count. 'Zero. Now!'

The screen died and, as it did, the engines of the Eagle flared to full power, the vessel rising to swing out and away from the danger of the cone, the defence shield glowing again as soon as the area was clear. A system designed to gain maximum protection and one, they all hoped, which would do just that.

On the planetoid Koenig watched as the Eagle landed. He stood on the smooth, curved surface, some distance from the shaft they had found, the ground all around littered with stacked boxes and equipment. Two other Eagles were grounded to one side and, as Carter's vessel landed, one of them lifted and headed back towards the Moon.

'Thomson?' Koenig spoke into his radio. 'Is that you?'

'Yes, Commander.'

'Remember to hand over to Riddle when you arrive. You've done three flights and that's enough.'

'I can manage, Commander.'

'You'll do as I order!' Koenig made no attempt to soften his tone. 'If you want to gain fifty years in a few minutes that's your concern, I'm worried about the Eagle. If you want to be a hero then do it without risking the ship. Understood?'

'Commander, I—'

'You're a fool,' Koenig interrupted. Then added, more softly, 'And Alpha needs all the fools like you it can get. I don't want to waste one. You've served your stint, man. Get back, put

Riddle in charge of the Eagle and report to Medical for checking. No arguments, now. Do it!'

He turned as the Eagle vanished from sight and stepped towards the head of the shaft. On all sides men were busy moving the crates, handling them with exaggerated care, never placing them too close to each other. At the head of the shaft technicians emptied the boxes and handed their contents down to others who moved them along the tunnels.

They had worked for hours like a horde of busy ants shifting scraps of leaves to form an underground farm. But these things they carried were not leaves and they would build no farm. Down in the chamber which held the dead aliens, buried deep beneath the surface and sealed by the stubborn metal, a tremendous bomb was in process of manufacture.

A fission bomb which would emulate the sun in its fury.

'John?' Bergman climbed slowly from the shaft, rising up a metal ladder which had made progress easier than the original hoops. His voice was fatigued, the way he moved betrayed his tiredness, the way he stood.

'How's it going?'

'Well, but—'

'Follow me. Let's get into Kendal's Eagle and take a break. You could do with some coffee.'

'I can manage.'

'You too?' Koenig grunted his irritation. 'The place is swarming with crazy idiots who want to work themselves to death. Come and get some coffee, Victor. That's an order.'

One Bergman was glad to obey. Later, sitting in the Eagle with a steaming cup of coffee in his hand, he admitted that he was tired.

'I'm not surprised,' said Koenig. 'How long has it been since you last slept?'

'About as long as you've been awake, John.'

'Which makes us two of a kind.' Koenig took a sip of his own coffee. 'How much longer will it be?'

He was talking of the bomb and Bergman knew it. He said, 'We've almost got everything into place down below. The initial fission device is set and now we're arranging the rest. It's a big charge, John.

'It needs to be.'

'But not big enough to volatise this planetoid.'

Koenig said, impatiently, 'I know that, Victor, but it doesn't have to. You worked out the figures and decided on the megaton-scale necessary. It's close but it will have to do.'

'I'd like another two loads set in place just to make sure.' Bergman produced his inevitable slide rule and manipulated it, forgetting his coffee in his sudden introspection. 'Two loads at least,' he decided. 'There are too many variables which we haven't been able to take into full account. The core, for example. It could be of unsuspected density.'

'We'll have to use what we've got, Victor.'

'But, John—'

'We have no choice. Did you know that three more have fallen from age-sickness?'

'I know, but the defence shield will prevent further cases.'

'As far as we know – but how can we be sure? The power may fail, the energy-beam take more than we can deliver, circumstances may change at any moment. We've got to act while we have the chance.'

Rising Koenig paced the confines of the passenger compartment. How to explain the fear which engulfed him? The conviction that already they were on borrowed time?

'Commander!' Kendal called from the command module. 'The Omphalos – come and look!'

It hung in space as he remembered, greenly glowing, marked with the dark tracery of lines which gave the appearance of convolutions, divided into the resemblance of a human brain.

And then it pulsed.

'John!' Bergman leaned towards the screen. 'It – It—'

How to describe the sudden inflation and deflation of apparently solid matter? The previously noted pulsations had been minor, the product of an interplay of light or the interpretation of a dazzled mind. But this had been no gentle undulation.

'God!' Kendal was a big man with no concept of personal

fear but now his voice held a strained terror. 'It moved! Commander – the damn thing's alive!'

The drugs were bitter to the taste, tablets which he swallowed and washed down with a sickly liquid. Dope to keep him awake and aware, to force tired musclese to respond, eyes to see, his brain to think.

'John, you shouldn't take all these things.' Helena had been reluctant to give them, yielding only to his direct order, his thinly veiled anger at her reluctance to obey. 'You'll pay for this later.'

'Sure – now don't bother me.'

'John—'

'Helena, we're fighting time. Give what drugs are needed and spare me your lectures. Don't you understand, woman? We're fighting for our lives!'

Against a thing which could not exist but, incredibly, did.

Koenig stared at it where it rested in the screens. Around him in Main Mission everyone seemed to be holding their breath, waiting, standing poised on the brink of extinction.

'The Omphalos has increased to one fifth its previous size,' Morrow reported. 'Is now pulsing at twice the rate observed at commencement.'

'Sandra?'

'Energy loss mounting, Commander. The rate is nearing totality.'

Complete absorption, the energy drained as fast as it was produced and when the defence shield went down all would be helplessly exposed to the aging action of the alien forces.

Time!

It was running against them, wasted by necessity, precious seconds turning into minutes, into hours.

How much longer did they have?

'What news from the Eagle, Paul?'

'On its way, Commander. All remaining personnel aboard together with Professor Bergman.'

'Have him report here as soon as he docks. Get me ground defence.' Koenig waited as an auxillary screen blurred to steady, to picture the taut face of a Security guard.

'Commander?'

'Report on readiness for action.'

'All as ordered. Tubes aimed and ready. Missiles primed and all warheads with treble charges.' Hesitating he added, 'If we fire as ordered we'll be stripped of all capability.'

'If you don't we'll be dead.'

Koenig shook his head as the screen darkened. Too many drugs taken too quickly had fogged his vision and etched at his self-control, but he'd had no choice and neither had the others. Morrow, red-eyed, face slack with weariness. Sandra, looking like a ghost, Kano a grim and silent figure, Helena, reproachful and yet helpless to do more than what she had.

And now she could do nothing but wait.

Wait as Carter's Eagle came into view, darting in to land as the screen lowered, settling as again the shield lifted, the lights dimming, almost dying, restored as Morrow adjusted his instruments.

Close – and the shield had lost its previous brilliance. Even now she could be growing old with accelerated speed, bones becoming brittle, blood thinning, glands withering, life and the lust for life drained and sucked by the alien thing to which this constricted universe belonged.

How long had it traversed space?

A tiny thing at the beginning, perhaps, feeding on energy, growing, developing, aware of food-sources, catching them with its beams, reducing them into energy which it stole. Eating them.

A roving parasite of the void.

A danger sealed into a place of its own by some race owning a tremendously high technology but lacking the inclination to destroy. Instead they had warped the very fabric of the continuum to form an escape-proof cage and had set it about with warnings as to what it contained.

'Victor!' Koenig turned as Bergman entered Main Mission and came towards him. 'Is everything ready?'

'Yes.' Bergman glanced at the chronometer. 'Firing commences in one hour thirty-three minutes.'

'So long?'

'The planetoid must be in the right position for the plan to work. Computer gave position and timing. Right, David?'

'Yes, Professor.' Kano rubbed at his reddened eyes. 'Any deviation from the plan will result in lost efficiency.'

A lowering of the already slim margin of potential success, but the odds against them were growing all the time. Koenig glanced at the dials, saw the needles edging towards the red, the warning flash of signal lights.

'Cut all unessential power to all areas, Paul.'

'I've saved all I can, Commander.'

'Save more. Switch to emergency battery power if you have to. Just remember that we'll need full power fed into the shield when we blow.'

Morrow acknowledged with a nod and Koenig moved to where Helena stood watching the screens. The greenish light, now a blazing flame, touched her face and accentuated the strong contours of jaw and cheeks, the wide-set of the eyes.

She whispered, 'That pulsing, John. It's like the pound of a heart.'

Or the kick of a child impatient to be born. Yet how could familiar concepts apply? The Omphalos was not a creature giving birth nor yet a creature being born. It was expanding, growing as an organic thing would grow, and yet it was not organic.

Koenig remembered the sensations he had experienced when lost in the illusions he had known while in close proximity to the green bulk. Had he experienced the stored knowledge of actual beings? The deaths – had they been actual memories of minds absorbed by the Omphalos?

A germ, he thought, caught in a human bloodstream, drawn to the brain, entrammelled in the cortex, sharing, in part, the stir and process of thought.

Did a man consider the fate of what he ate?

Would he care if it was aware?

'Thirteen minutes, Commander.' Sandra Benes was tense, uneasily aware of the superstition connected to the number.

Now, if at all, any bad luck would surely become manifest. Despite her resolution not to look she lifted her eyes to where the main screen depicted the Omphalos. It was twice its original size now, pulsating, greenly malevolent. A predator poised and ready to strike. A bomb on the edge of explosion.

'Sandra!'

Morrow had been watching her and at the sound of his voice she started, dropping her eyes from the hypnotic image, concentrating again on her instruments.

'Sorry, Paul.'

'Time?'

'Eleven minutes,' At least the unlucky number had been safely passed. 'Energy loss mounting. Some traces of temperature differential noted from the central body.'

'High?' Bergman fired the question.

'No. It's varying from zero to twelve degrees celsius.'

'Any radiation?'

'Slight traces, Professor, but our own energy-loss is affecting the readings.'

'But they are positive?'

Bergman grunted as she nodded. To Koenig he said, 'You realise what this means, John? The external layers of the Omphalos must be splitting. The result, perhaps, of the massive increase in its energy-intake since we entered its space. It is obviously adapting to meet the new circumstances.'

'Growing?'

'In a sense, John, yes. As a crystal will grow when immersed in a super-saturated solution. It is a sponge absorbing energy, using it to build up its mass, adding to its reserves. Later, if all sources of energy should be denied to it, then the reverse process will apply. It will shrink as it consumes its own bulk. Men do the same, John. And stars. It seems to be a universal law.'

Eat or starve.

Grow or wither.

Kill or die!

Koenig glanced at the screens, the instruments facing Morrow where he sat, the tell-tales and monitors of the consol. The base was on red alert, ground defences standing by, engineers ready to wring the last erg of power from generators and to maintain a maximum flow no matter what the cost.

'Three minutes.' Sandra's voice betrayed her strain. 'Two and a half. Two.'

Now only a hundred seconds to wait . . . ninety . . . eighty . . . seventy . . .

Koenig felt Helena at his side and turned his head to smile reassurance.

'Soon now.'

'John! If it doesn't work!'

'It will! It must!'

Their only chance and, if it failed, death would be waiting. A gamble with their lives as the stake.

'Ten!' Sandra began to count the seconds. At the consol Morrow sent signals to the waiting men. Bergman, eyes narrowed, stared at the glowing mass of the Omphalos. Kano gently stroked a panel as if giving comfort to his beloved computer.

Koenig felt his face harden and grow wet with oozing sweat.

He had to be right.

Had to!

'Three . . . Two . . . One . . . Now!' A moment then Sandra said, bleakly, 'It isn't working. It isn't going to work!'

'Wait!' Bergman turned from the screen. 'We can't see anything as yet and your instruments can't pick up what lies behind the Omphalos. Paul?'

'Booster signals sent, Professor, but the automatics should have fired by now.'

The time fuses planted with the massed nuclear materials in the body of the planetoid. Heaped in mathematical precision in the chamber of alien dead. A tremendous bomb which flashed to life in an eye-searing halo about the Omphalos.

A wide circle of savage, blue-white glare which dulled the green. Which spread to form a backdrop of sun-like fury.

'It worked!' Bergman shouted his relief. 'John! It worked!'

The fuses, yes. The nuclear bomb itself, yes. But the rest? A flood of raw radiation, by itself, wouldn't have been enough. The Omphalos ate energy, it used it, lived on it, sucked it in. At the distance, savage though it was, the atomic explosion would have been of limited use. But there had been more.

The planetoid with its shafts and mass. The chamber which had held the bomb, the blasting explosion which had torn the remnants of what had once been a habitated world apart, fragments which even now, if the calculations had been correct, were hurtling towards the green menace.

A blast of matter which would rip into the Omphalos with the impact of a shotgun blast against a bag of water.

Matter which would be converted into energy on contact, each grain of dust, every fragment, in turn an atomic explosion.

'Paul! Fire all missiles!'

Morrow nodded at Koenig's command and relayed the order. From the launching tubes ringing the base slender shapes lanced into space; torpedoes loaded with a treble charge of atomic destruction in their heads, their drive mechanisms rigged to gain maximum velocity at the expense of accuracy.

The target was too big to be missed.

Morrow said, anxiously, 'Commander! The shield?'

'Wait!'

There was time yet and every second was precious. Koenig stood, mentally counting, visualising what was happening in space. The flight of the massed torpedoes, the paths taken by the masses torn from the disrupted planetoid. They would strike together, a double-blow in opposed synchronisation and, when they did, the Omphalos would die.

The alien mass would be destroyed, disintegrated, bathed with a flood of energy so intense that it could not be stored or utilised.

'Commander?'

'Not yet.'

'But, John!' Bergman too was anxious. 'If—'

'Wait!'

A knife-edged calculation. Raise the defence shield to full strength too soon and the energy would be drained to leave them defenceless against the moment of need. Wait too long and they too would be blasted by the floor of raw destruction soon to fill the enclosed area of this miniature universe.

On the screen the Omphalos flickered, seemed to jerk, to swell, to expand with frightening speed.

'Now, Paul! Now!'

The blaze of the defence shield matched the fury of the heavens, the dazzle of scintillating particles blasting the eyes with a mass of kaleidoscopic coruscations.

For a long moment there was silence then Helena said, 'John, is it holding?'

'Sandra?'

'Energy loss mounting towards total drain. Still climbing.' Her voice quivered a little and the knuckles of her hands where they gripped the edge of the panel shone white. 'Climbing. Climbing – no, steadying now. Steady and falling. Falling! Commander – we're safe!'

Safe behind the protection of the shield as the naked fury of disrupted atoms streamed around them, filling all space with a maelstrom of tormented energies, stresses mounting, conflicting, tearing at the very fabric of the continuum until something had to yield.

When it did it was like the snapping of an overstraned rubber band.

Koenig felt a jerk, a sudden movement of the floor beneath his feet, a shudder which ran through the base, then heard Bergman's starteled cry.

'Look! The stars! The stars!'

The screen was full of them; bright, coldly remote but comforting in their familiarity. Space was normal again, the bubble which had held them prisoner broken and dissolved.

They were free and, of the Omphalos, nothing remained but a dying smear of fading emerald – the pyre of a destroyed world.

1 465